one week to win her boss

The Snowflake Valley Series

one week to win her boss

The Snowflake Valley Series

BARBARA WHITE DAILLE

This book is a work of fiction. Names, characters, places, and incidents are the product of the author's imagination or are used fictitiously. Any resemblance to actual events, locales, or persons, living or dead, is coincidental.

Entangled Publishing, LLC
2614 South Timberline Road
Suite 105, PMB 159
Fort Collins, CO 80525
Visit our website at www.entangledpublishing.com.

Bliss is an imprint of Entangled Publishing, LLC.
For more information on our titles, visit http://www.entangledpublishing.com/category/bliss

Edited by Alycia Tornetta
Cover design by Cora Graphics
Cover art from Shutterstock

Manufactured in the United States of America

First Edition November 2017

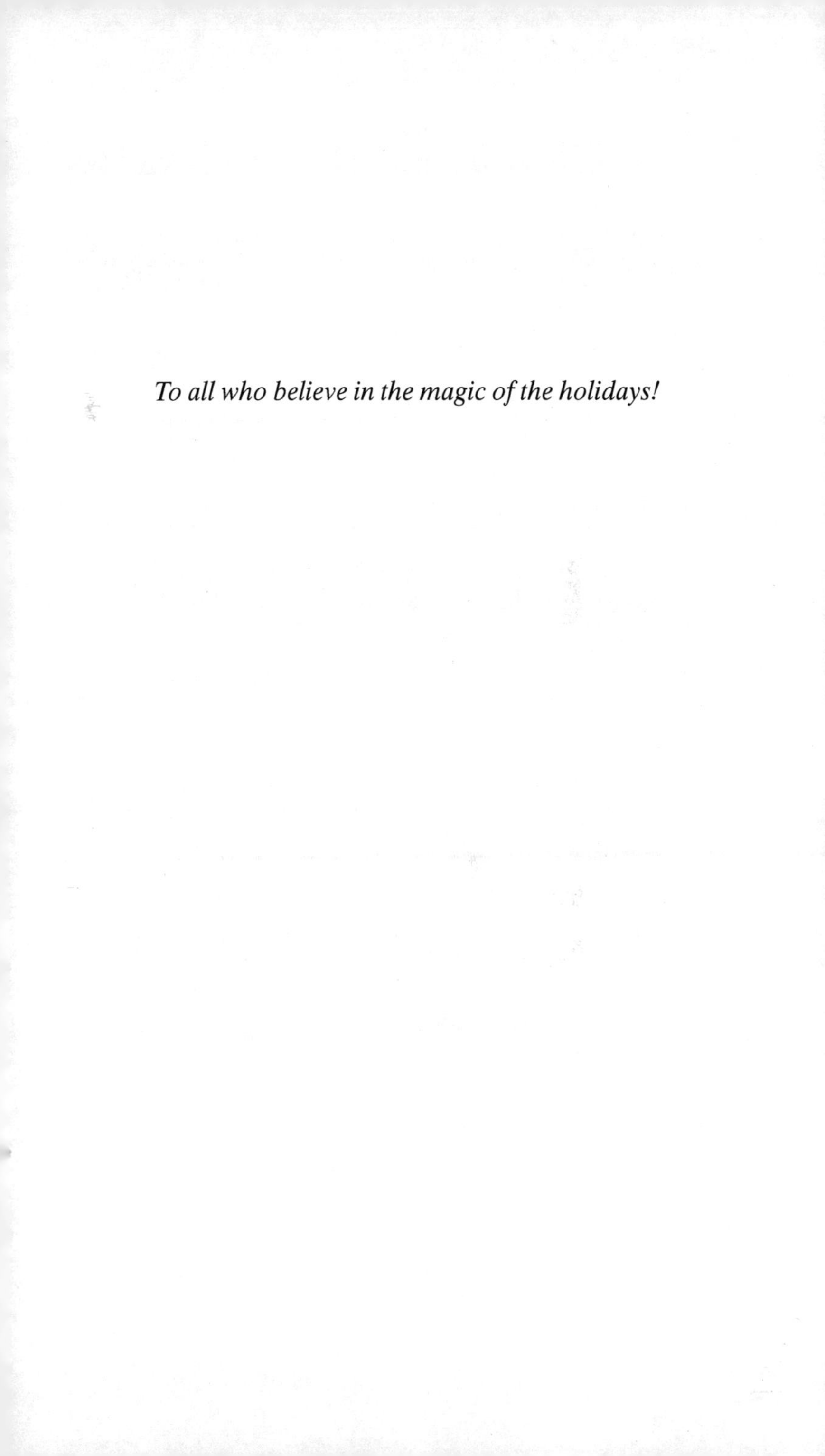

To all who believe in the magic of the holidays!

Chapter One

The jingling of Santa's sleigh bells jolted Amber Barnett awake on the couch. Following the bells came a thud, a crash, a clatter, and a long string of muttered curses. That couldn't be. Santa wouldn't swear like a sailor, especially not on Christmas Eve.

Time to wake up. She was hearing things and not making any sense. Well, it *had* been a long, stressful trip here. With the storm racing toward Snowflake Valley, heading up to her boss's mountain lodge after her family's open house might not have been the brightest idea ever. But it was the best solution she could come up with.

She glanced at the small playpen near one end of the couch. In the dim light from the table lamp, her four-month-old daughter lay looking up at her peacefully, unbothered by whatever Amber thought she'd heard.

Amber leaned down to tuck Penny's lightweight blanket around her. "We left later than planned," she murmured, "and the snowstorm was worse than I expected. And okay, maybe we shouldn't have come here at all." She looked around the large living room she had decorated for the holidays only a week ago. "But it's not like I had much of a choice. The mean old electric company turned off our service. It was either hide out here for a few days, or go to Grandma and Grandpa's house and face everyone."

Right. And let Callie and Lyssa know she had screwed up—yet again.

The thought made her shudder. Her older sisters loved her and she loved them. But living with their tendency to fly to her rescue? Not so much to like there. It was as if they both felt they couldn't trust her to do anything right.

Her ex's attitude had been even worse. With him, there was no *seemed* about it. He told her outright and on a regular basis she needed him to take care of everything. Another good reason she now called him her ex.

A loud thump made her heart leap.

Those noises she'd heard *hadn't* come from a dream.

Someone was in the kitchen.

It couldn't be her boss. Michael was spending the holidays with his family in California.

The footsteps grew louder. He—or she—was getting closer to her and her daughter. *Scoop up Penny and run.* But the car keys were in her room. She would never reach the stairs in time. And even if she could make it as far as the front door, how could she escape on foot in a snowstorm?

Nobody's getting between me and my baby. She grabbed a heavy ornament sitting on the coffee table.

The footsteps came even nearer to the door.

Swallowing a shriek, she raced across the room and past the dining area. Her slippers padded silently on the wooden floor.

As she reached the doorway, her weapon held high, a towering man stepped through the opening. Recognition hit—too late. Fear and adrenaline had her in full swing. The ornament zeroed in on her boss's snow-frosted head.

Michael lunged, reaching up to wrench the weapon from her hands. "What the…? *Amber*?"

Well, one consolation—if you could call it that—he looked as shaken up as she felt. The reply whooshed from her mind straight to her mouth. "You're not supposed to be here!"

"Neither are *you*. And especially not armed for battle. I didn't mean to scare you. Heck, if I'd known you were here, I'd have called ahead, if only to keep you from trying to knock me out with a…with a…" He looked down at the ornament in his hand. "A *troll*?"

"It's not a troll. It's an elf. A *Christmas* elf."

"Oh. Well. That makes it all right, then, doesn't it?"

Her laugh shook so badly, it rattled. "Well, after all, it *is* Christmas Eve."

He grimaced. "Yeah, I got that memo. But not the one about why you're here."

Frantically, she tried to figure out how to explain to her boss she had become a squatter in his private ski lodge. And as always when she really needed an idea, not even a glimmer of one hit.

As Michael walked over to set the ornament on the banquet-sized dining room table, her heart gave an unsteady thump. She had met him a little over a year ago, at this very lodge when she had come for her interview. One look at him had left her breathless.

She took a quick peek. Nope, nothing had changed. He still had those snapping dark-brown eyes surrounded by thick, dark lashes. Broad shoulders. Muscular arms. And when he had shaken her hand that day, his warm, strong fingers wrapped almost protectively around hers. To top it off, he had the sexiest deep voice she had ever heard.

All those drool-worthy qualities explained her immediate attraction. *Any* woman would have fallen for Michael

DeFranco on the spot.

She would never have taken the man for the owner of an electronics company. Her brothers teased her about working for a techno-nerd. That name didn't come close to doing Michael justice. Privately, she thought of him as her own personal geek god. A silly idea. Just the right match for her equally stupid instant crush. A crush she had already set a New Year's resolution to ditch.

Nobody was perfect, not even Michael. Though he sure looked darned close...but then, how would she know? Above all else, her time with her ex had proven she couldn't trust her judgment when it came to men.

"Come back down to Earth, Amber." She jumped. Michael stood in front of her, too close for comfort. "When you land, tell me why you're here. And in your pajamas."

His almost seductive growl did funny things to her insides. Too bad the question hadn't slipped his mind, the way she'd forgotten what she was wearing—a floor-length, fuzzy, pink bathrobe that had seen better days and floppy-eared bunny slippers no one but she and Penny had ever seen. Nothing like making a fashion statement.

Hopefully, he would be more impressed by her response to his question—as soon as she thought of one. "I...um... didn't ask if you would mind if I stayed here—"

"That's obvious."

"—because I didn't expect you to drop in."

"Twice as obvious." His gaze ran over her from head to toe.

Her body flooded with heat she wished she could blame on the warm robe. Why couldn't she and Penny have had somewhere—*anywhere*—else to stay? "What are *you* doing here, by the way?"

"I own the place."

She rolled her eyes. "You said you were spending the

holidays with your family."

"Yeah. Huge mistake," he said, sounding grim as he looked away.

What did that mean? She wanted to know more about his upset holiday plans and his visit with his family. She'd never met them and had always been curious about why they'd never visited the lodge. Besides, she wanted to know *everything* there was to know about Michael.

Way to get over that crush.

Time to take control of this situation. No matter how inconvenient his arrival was for her or how unsettling his presence was to her heart, the fact was, there he stood. If she wanted to save her job—and she absolutely did—she owed him an explanation. Or at least part of one.

"I need a place to stay, just for a few days," she said truthfully. "And I don't want my family to find out."

"Interesting." He tilted his head, studying her, making her heart skip a beat. "Do you do this often?"

"No! I've never stayed here before. Except when you've asked me to. When you've come here with guests, I mean." *Get a grip. Falling apart won't impress your boss any more than the bunny slippers did.* Taking a tip from her birthing class, she inhaled and exhaled a deep, calming breath and tried again. "Michael, I've never stayed here on my own before. And I wouldn't have done it without asking you this time. But I knew you had plans for the holidays, and I didn't want to bother you while you were with your family."

"Believe me, I'd have welcomed the bother." His scowl sent her curiosity skyrocketing. "I don't mind that you didn't ask. It's good to have the house occupied once in a while. I just didn't expect company."

"I'll keep out of your way," she promised.

One dark eyebrow rose as he stared her down. "Somehow, I don't see that leading to the peace and quiet—

and solitude—I was looking for."

"No worries. Hand to heart." She rested her palm against her chest. The fuzzy robe tickled her fingers. When his gaze followed her movement, she froze. Had she just seen a spark of interest in his eyes? Right. More like a vision from her own pitiful wishful thinking. She shoved her hand into the pocket of the robe. "I'll stay far away," she promised again. "You won't hear a peep out of me."

At that moment, as if on cue, Penny let out her usual I'm-ready-to-eat screech. Michael's suddenly blank expression proved he had heard the baby, too, and wasn't pleased. *But wait—there's more.* Penny's hunger cries were loud enough. How would he handle her being colicky?

"What was that?" he demanded.

"Uh…not what. Who. My daughter." Michael had never met Penny. In fact, he hadn't even known about Amber's pregnancy until she was so far along he couldn't miss the baby bump.

"Ah," he said. "When it comes to not making a peep, it doesn't look like you were speaking for your daughter."

She smiled sheepishly. "Sometimes she likes to speak for herself."

He shook his head, but his mouth curved up at one corner. He was fighting a smile. Even in the midst of this disaster, even with the recent reminder that she couldn't and shouldn't trust her judgment around men, that half-smile was enough to make her melt.

So not good. But the thought of having him upset with her had been more than her stressed-out, worried, and exhausted mind could handle.

Penny let out her feed-me-*now* screech. Guaranteed, one of those cries could send a zombie scrambling back into his grave.

This time, Michael winced.

"I should go get her." Amber edged toward the living room. "She needs to be fed."

Another screech.

He nodded. "I think she's voted yes on that." He backed a step. "Guess I'll go and unpack."

"Sounds good." *Good?* No, it sounded more like Michael had decided to get out of range of Penny. And maybe of her, too?

• • •

Upstairs in the bedroom of the lodge's master suite, Michael tossed his suitcase on the bed. So much for the visit to his dad's. Most of the clothes had never left the case. He had expected to stay only a few days, maximum, but had cut the trip even shorter than that.

And then he'd come here to find Amber lying in wait. Christmas elf or no Christmas elf, one look at her had thrown him—almost as forcibly as the day they'd met. Then, he'd instantly come up with plenty of reasons to ask her out. Dark honey-brown hair tumbling over her shoulders. Bright blue eyes. Curves even her bulky blue sweater couldn't hide. What item on that list wouldn't grab a man's interest?

With a grunt of disgust, he tossed his jacket onto the bed beside the suitcase. On his way downstairs he gave himself a familiar reminder: *Amber is off-limits.*

Outside the kitchen door he hesitated, taking a deep breath. Mama DeFranco would have scolded him in three different languages for the way he had sworn at Amber when he'd come into the house. But guilt instilled by his grandmother wasn't what kept him hanging outside in the hallway. No, it was his eagerness to join Amber that rooted his feet to the floor. Better for him to stand out here than to be alone with her.

A wail went up inside the kitchen.

With her and her baby, he amended.

In one corner of the kitchen, the infant lay in the playpen Amber must have moved from the living room.

She stood at the counter. She had shed her robe, revealing a soft-looking yellow sweater skimming her waist and a pair of jeans hugging her hips. His mouth watered. And no matter how he tried, he couldn't connect that reaction to the appetizing smell of coffee filling the kitchen.

As if she'd heard his thoughts, she frowned. "I hope you won't be too disappointed."

"Me? Never." He cleared his throat and brought his voice down a few octaves. "Ah…disappointed by what?"

"I still have coffee on the hot plate. But the fridge is nearly empty. If you want something to eat, you'll have to settle for eggs or canned soup. Or a plate of my mom's leftovers."

"I'll pass for tonight. But for the record, leftovers are my favorite meal."

Her laugh was exactly the response he'd gone for. Instead, he should have been focused on finding out why she was here. He followed her movements from the counter to the fridge and back again. As her employer, he should have been noticing her competence in the kitchen.

Not even close.

From the playpen, her daughter babbled for a bit. Probably saying *You'd better watch yourself, mister.*

He darned sure would.

At the time he'd met Amber, he had been clueless about her pregnancy. But even before they'd gone their separate ways that day, his interest in her had kicked off a craving he wanted to satisfy. Stupid thinking, when he had no intention of getting involved with a woman like her, a woman who had one big flaw, at least as far as he was concerned.

She had already started a family.

He'd had his fill of raising his brothers, who added a few new twists to the word dysfunctional. Seeing how some of them had turned out, no way did he want to risk going through that again with kids of his own.

Amber's daughter and Amber's dedication to her family were the deal breakers for him. The steps he wouldn't take. The places he wouldn't go.

And so, he'd made a mental note: *Scratch her name off the Dating Potential list. Permanently.*

Yet on his visits here with a houseful of business associates, he always found time to talk with her. To check up on the lodge and the property… Yeah, sure. The truth was, there had always been something drawing him to Amber. Something different about her from all the other women he knew. Something enticing him close to a line he couldn't cross.

As he had no guests with him this visit, he'd also had no intention of asking her to work. Didn't take a brain surgeon to understand he'd wanted to avoid temptation.

"Earth to *Michael* this time," she said. "Were you able to park in the garage?"

"Barely, thanks to all the snow." Good thing the rental place at the airport had an oversized vehicle with snow tires on hand. "Does that stuff ever stop in Snowflake Valley?"

The grin she sent him shot his pulse up a few dozen notches. "Only when we turn off the giant snowmaking machine."

He laughed. "I always knew this place was too good to be true."

"No, it's not." She sounded shocked. "Snowflake Valley is perfect."

"Maybe for some. Considering the weather, I'm surprised you wanted to make the trip all the way up here. You couldn't have found someone to put you up for a night or two?" No answer. Even from this distance, he saw her face turn pink. She had told him she'd needed a place to stay "for a few days." For all he knew, she'd camped out here for weeks. Not that he cared. But why the big secret? "If you've been kicked out of your apartment—"

"I didn't get kicked out," she said quickly. "I was looking for peace and quiet—and solitude."

Yeah. In my lodge. "That makes two of us." Grinning, he added, "And yes, I caught my own words thrown back at me."

She hadn't told him the full story yet. One way or another, he'd make sure he found out what was going on. As her employer, he had an obligation to watch out for her, didn't he? But that could wait. Nobody was going back down that mountain in the snow at this hour.

On the floor beside the back door sat a paper grocery sack. He'd nearly broken his leg stumbling over it when he entered. "About what else I said earlier. Excuse the swearing. I was still off-balance from your warm welcome."

"The elf probably had something to do with that. Sorry." Flushing again, she reached up to run her hand through her hair. The long strands shifted against the front of her sweater.

Something inside him shifted, too. Fighting the urge to wrap his arms around her and kiss her senseless, he grabbed the twine handles of the sack. *Deep breath, man. Keep this light.* "Since you thought I was breaking in, I won't press charges."

"Since I was protecting your property, that's very generous of you."

Her teasing smile would've been worth getting decked by that elf. "Consider it a Christmas gift." He hefted the bag. "This feels heavier than it looks. What is it, your arsenal of backup weapons?"

She laughed. "No, that's just the canned soup I offered you."

"Who needs soup when you've got leftovers?"

"No one. So don't let my mom or sisters hear about it. I wasn't feeling well earlier, so I stopped at the store for a few things. Just in case I'm not up to either Christmas dinner *or* party leftovers tomorrow."

"Do you need to see a doctor?"

She shook her head. "No, I'm fine now, I think. Anyway, I'm also sorry about leaving the sack there. Once I got here, all I could think about was putting on my robe to get warm."

He could think of other ways to accomplish that. But the suggestion would probably get his face slapped. "You're welcome to stay tonight, too. But if your symptoms hit again, you'll be in big trouble. A can opener I can handle. I'd have to pass when it comes to taking care of a baby."

Because I'm never doing that again.

He also wasn't going to give in to his desire to kiss Amber, which increased with every minute he spent in her company.

For both their sakes, she had to go. Tomorrow, he'd see if she could find somewhere else to camp out. Meanwhile, he'd make the best of a bad situation, doubled. A sick mom and a screeching baby. The two things in this world he felt least ready to handle.

"Penny and I are having dinner with my family tomorrow," Amber said. "You're welcome to come along."

Make that three things.

"As my dad always says," she went on, "'the more the merrier—especially on Christmas Day.' And you won't want to be here all by yourself."

If she only knew. He shrugged. "No big deal. Just another day. Same as New Year's."

"You're staying till then?"

"I have an early flight on the second." Her eyes widened. Not in pleased surprise, as he might have suspected—and maybe welcomed. No, the expression in those blue eyes radiated dismay. What the heck did the woman have planned for this lodge?

"An entire week," she said faintly. "What about your business?"

Yeah, the business. The electronics company he had built from the ground up. The same one his lack of enthusiasm threatened to run right into that ground again. Not a subject he wanted to discuss. "It's closed until the new year. My office staff can reach me if needed." He stayed in touch by way of texts and emails, using all the technology he never traveled without. "But I don't expect them to have the need."

He glanced from Amber to Penny and back again. He hadn't expected them, either. After the disaster at his dad's house, he'd driven right to the lodge, planning to close and lock the door behind him. He hadn't intended to see or speak to anyone until the beginning of next year. If then.

As if she'd read his thoughts again, she said, "I'm sorry something happened to spoil your family holiday."

He laughed shortly. "*Family holiday.* An oxymoron, isn't that what they call it when two halves of a phrase contradict each other? Definitely a load of contradictions in that house."

"With only three of you there? It's just you and your dad and your stepmom, isn't it?"

"And a whole gang of half-brothers and stepbrothers. Believe me, spending time with my stepmother and her kids is no kind of holiday. I suffer through it for my dad's sake."

At least, he tried. Today's final straw had driven him from the house. His inability to handle the situation only stirred up memories of years ago, when he'd had even less control over the bad times in his life.

When his own mom had gotten sick, his dad and Mama DeFranco had taken care of her. He'd wanted to help but had been too young to do much of anything. To this day the thought of his helplessness ate at him.

A few years after his mom was gone, his dad had remarried. Once Carmen moved in along with her kids, he'd had plenty of time around babies. Too much time. He'd been in grade school, still a kid himself, still missing his own mom. But his stepmother hadn't tried to mother him at all. Instead, almost from day one, she had put him in charge of his stepbrothers and later his half-brothers.

"Living with that bunch was no picnic, either," he said. "I couldn't wait for the day I headed off to college and left them behind."

"You didn't visit them at all?" She sounded shocked.

"When I could force myself to go. It was always the same waste of time. Or worse. Today's shouting match over lunch was a perfect example." He shrugged. "But those visits all have a positive spin. They remind me why I don't want a family of my own."

Amber stood staring at him. In the middle of that silence, her daughter let out the most ear-piercing shriek he'd heard from her yet. He started, darned near dropping the sack of soup cans he'd been carrying to the counter.

How could such a small baby make such a racket? He had plenty of memories of crying kids, but none of the boys had reached *that* decibel level. "You just fed her. She can't be hungry again."

"That's not a hunger cry." Amber hurried over to the playpen. "She has colic."

"Does she have it often?"

"Too often, I'm sad to say. But it's chronic, not constant. And she's improving every day. Aren't you, sweetie?" She lifted the baby and settled her against her shoulder. "She'll feel better again. Soon."

The line between Amber's eyebrows told him not to start counting the minutes.

Chapter Two

Before the sun poked its head above the mountain peak the next morning, Amber tiptoed down to the living room. Step one of her easy-peasy plan. Keep Penny amused and quiet. Keep Michael happy.

She kissed Penny's forehead before kneeling to settle her in the playpen. "There you go, sweetie-pie." She stroked Penny's downy-soft cheek. She loved her daughter, heart and soul. Tears still stung her eyes every time she remembered how Penny's daddy hadn't wanted her.

When she had announced the news of her pregnancy to her husband, she hadn't expected to celebrate on her own. But they had argued, and he had stormed out. Hours later, his missing cell phone charger gave her the first clue he had left for good. She hadn't let that break her. She was on her own, but not alone. She'd had her baby on the way and her stubborn pride to hold onto.

"I don't know what I'd have done if I hadn't heard Michael was hiring," she told Penny. Suddenly single again and pregnant, she had been desperate to find a better-paying job to support them both. Hearing Michael was about to head back to California, she had grabbed the narrow window of opportunity just before it could slam shut. And the rest, she felt certain, was a Snowflake Valley miracle.

"No one needs to look out for me anymore, Penny," she said. "Not that man who left us. Not your Aunt Callie and Aunt Lyssa. I'm your mommy, and I'm here to take care of *you*." She smiled. "And you remember that house I told you about?" That someday-some-way-gonna-buy-it house… "Soon, I'll save up enough money so we can live in our own home instead of that tiny apartment. Enough money to keep from ever missing a bill payment again."

She sighed. "Of course, that never would have happened if your mommy wasn't such a pushover." If she hadn't emptied her bank account for a friend's emergency.

But she would recoup her losses with her next paycheck, which was one of the biggest reasons she had wanted to become the caretaker-slash-housekeeper of Michael DeFranco's private ski lodge. Job openings in Snowflake Valley came few and far between. Ones that paid as much as he had offered for the easy part-time hours were practically unheard-of. That generous pay would make her dream house a reality someday.

As for her other dreams…

"I confess, that morning we met, I went tumbling head-over-heels."

It wasn't surprising she had fallen so quickly—and it had nothing to do with being on the rebound. "The last thing I wanted was another man on my mind. But then"—she lowered her voice to a murmur—"I met *that* man."

Michael's hot looks aside, she had a second, secret list of what had drawn her to him like a downhill racer to the finish line.

But even that didn't come close to the rest of the items

on her very long list. She loved that he found his way to her whenever she stayed at the lodge, even though he had guests to entertain. She loved how he listened to what she had to say, how he laughed when she shared one of her brothers' not-so-funny jokes. And she loved the way he made her feel, all butterflies-cartwheeling-in-her-stomach and as breathless as a teen on her first date.

Most of all, when she looked at Michael, she loved seeing the perfect daddy for Penny. And the perfect man for her.

Of course, when Michael looked at her, what did he see? A housekeeper.

She needed to remember that.

In the dim light from the table lamp, the baby closed her eyes. Amber slowly rose and backed away from the playpen. She curled up on the couch and covered herself with the afghan she had left there the night before.

Overhead, the sound of footsteps hit the landing, then Michael descended the open, soaring staircase. Her heart soared, too, proving she shouldn't stay here at the lodge another night. But *shouldn't* and *wouldn't* were such different things.

"Morning," he said easily.

She put a finger to her lips. "Merry Christmas," she whispered.

Michael came closer. "Why are we whispering?" he asked. Mesmerizing brown eyes stared into hers.

"Uh-h-h..." *What?* She shook her head. "Penny's asleep. She hasn't made it through a night without waking up in forever."

"And so neither has her mom?"

His insight made her eyes fill with tears. Blinking, she forced a laugh. "Well, let's just say, fingers crossed and this being Christmas, maybe tonight Santa will bring us both the gift of sleep."

"I doubt even Santa can work a miracle like that one. But we can hope." He'd kept his voice low, and the husky murmur seemed to vibrate through her. "Want me to light the fire?"

"That's my job."

"Not today, it isn't."

This wasn't at all the way she had expected to spend her Christmas morning. But what could be better than being with Michael again.

She hadn't seen him since he had brought some friends for a ski vacation at Thanksgiving. As on his previous visits, he had asked her to stay at the lodge, filling in as both housekeeper and cook. Once Penny was born, she had always left her with her parents. Today was the first time she had brought the baby with her.

And Michael didn't want either of them here.

Done with the fire, he said, "Did I smell coffee on my way downstairs?"

"Yes. It's brewed by now. I'll get it."

When she began to push the afghan away, he reached out to stop her. His touch made her hand tingle. She wanted to turn her palm up and twine her fingers through his, to tug him down onto the couch beside her. Which made no sense. Hadn't she spent half the night reminding herself to keep her distance?

Abruptly, he pulled his hand away and headed toward the kitchen.

Her cheeks burned, and not from the fire. Considering her thoughts, *longing* had to have been written all over her face. A longing for him she would never get to satisfy. What if he'd read it in her expression or seen it in her eyes? What if she'd just ruined her and her daughter's future for a six-second fantasy fueled by her stupid crush?

Shivering, she pulled the afghan up to her chin. Sap from the logs exploded with crackles and pops, filling the silence in the room. Too bad it couldn't drown out the thoughts now filling her head, the ones she had spent the *other* half of the night trying to forget. *As if.*

How could she *not* remember what Michael had said about his visits home?

They remind me why I don't want a family of my own.

With those words, she had sworn she'd heard her heart break.

All her life, she had dreamed of settling down and raising a family. A family she had already begun with Penny. And if all went as planned, her daughter would have many brothers and sisters.

She needed to focus on that dream—and forget her crazy feelings for Michael.

• • •

When Michael returned to the living room carrying a tray, Amber pushed the afghan aside. She would sit up and act naturally. Well, as naturally as she could with her pulse beating so loudly she was sure he could hear it. "You don't have to wait on me."

"The first one to pour coffee in the morning also gets to serve it. One of Mama's rules."

"Your mom?"

"Grandmother. My dad's mom. Everybody called her Mama DeFranco." He took a seat on the leather armchair opposite her. "She lived with us until she passed away, when I was about nine. And Mama didn't take flak from any of us when it came to her kitchen rules. Neither will I. So drink your coffee, no complaining."

He smiled, maybe to soften his statement. It definitely made her feel all soft and gooey inside. "If you're turning on your charm, you're wasting your time," she lied. "I'm immune to it."

"I doubt that. I've heard it's so potent, they've made a vaccine especially to protect women against it."

She laughed. "Funny, but I've never heard a thing about that. And why haven't I ever heard any of Mama's kitchen rules before? Were you afraid I'd set a few of my own?"

"Yep. And trust me, I'm no waiter. You wouldn't want me trying to serve coffee to a houseful of guests."

But he'd just served it to her. Her soft-and-gooey insides threatened to melt into a puddle.

This was dangerous, her crazy thinking added to his... flirting? Could Michael possibly be *flirting* with her? She turned to the playpen and adjusted the blanket she had spread across Penny.

"She still asleep?" he asked.

Was he worried about his peace and quiet? "Yes. And once she's finally out, not much fazes her."

"Why should it? She knows all she has to do is wake up. Then one yell, and she'll get whatever she wants."

She laughed. Let him pretend irritation all he wanted. She'd seen his smile last night. "You have to admit, I'm training her well."

"You do everything well."

Flushing at the compliment, she focused on taking a sip of coffee.

"That's why I keep you on the payroll," he added.

Her pleasure dimmed. No pretense now. No flirting smile. His meaning couldn't have come across any clearer if he'd announced it in an email, the way they usually communicated. He thought of her as the hired help. Which she was, of course. Too bad she couldn't remember that. But no, despite all her warnings, she kept hoping she was more to him than the woman who cleaned his house. She kept daydreaming about him becoming more than her boss.

New Year's and that resolution of hers couldn't come soon enough.

Michael crossed the room to shift a log in the fireplace. The fire reminded her of the disaster-that-wouldn't-quit, otherwise known as her electric bill. How could she and Penny live in the apartment without heat in this weather?

She couldn't stay at the lodge with Michael here. But where else could she go?

Run home to her family? No way. She refused to let them know she wasn't the independent, in-control single mom she wanted them to see.

She trusted all her friends but couldn't ask for their help. Even if not a single one of them talked, everyone in Snowflake Valley would eventually know what had happened. One person would see something, another would overhear something else, and before she knew it, she would have no secrets from anyone, including Michael.

He took his seat again and looked at her. "Amber, what are you hiding from your family?"

She clamped her coffee mug in a death grip. "Who said I was hiding anything from them?" she asked cautiously.

"You did. You said not to tell your mom and sisters about the soup."

"Oh. That." She forced a laugh. "They would disown me for not making it from scratch. They're all very into homemade food, homemade clothes...homemade *everything.* Callie, my oldest sister—you met her, she's the one who's a teacher. Anyway, she even has a recipe to make her own Christmas ornaments out of paste and flour."

He eyed the tree in the corner of the room. Needing some Christmas cheer, she had turned the lights on when she'd come downstairs with Penny.

"Don't worry," she said, "I decorated it myself, and I promise you there's not a handmade ornament in the bunch."

"Hey, I already told you, I couldn't care less. It's your tree, not mine. If it were up to me, there wouldn't be one in the house."

"Scrooge," she teased. Instant conversation stopper. No return smile from him, as she had hoped. No comment, either. Just a silent shrug.

She needed to keep him away from the topic of secrets. "By the way," she said in a rush, "thank you again for letting me hold the party here. It was a big hit—again."

Last year, he had loaned the lodge to her for the annual Christmas party she organized for the kids of Snowflake Valley. Since she had only worked for him a couple of months, she had been touched by his generous offer. This year, she'd gotten another go-ahead. The party earlier in the week seemed like a lifetime ago. And like the only thing that had gone right for her in ages. "We had to cut the festivities short to escape the blizzard. Other than that, everyone had a great time."

He raised an eyebrow. "Including Santa?"

"Now, that's a different story." Michael had either conned or coerced the same friend who had played Santa last year into returning for this year's party. "You should have seen Nick's face when he discovered who was playing Miss Elf again." She stared down at her coffee. "I was sorry you had to back out at the last minute. You would have made a great Santa yourself."

"Santa? *Me?*" He laughed. "*Bah, humbug.*"

His mocking tone surprised her. "You *are* a Scrooge, aren't you? That's so sad. Christmas is my favorite holiday."

"Good thing for you, since there's no getting away from it around here."

She smiled wryly. "I can't argue with that. Not when I live and work in a town called Snowflake Valley. As Mayor Corrigan would tell you"—she attempted to mimic his deep voice—"'three-hundred-and-sixty-five days a year, we cater to tourists celebrating the season.' But you have to admit Christmas is a magical time. And I'm glad that magic brought Santa and Miss Elf their happy-ever-after." The fact that Miss Elf was her sister made the good news even more special.

When he frowned, obviously puzzled, she smiled. "I forgot. You wouldn't have heard the news yet. Lyssa and Nick are engaged."

Michael snorted a laugh.

"What's so funny?"

"Just reacting to the idea of Nick getting married."

"Because you never thought he'd find the right girl?"

"No. Because I thought he was smart enough to know marriage isn't a winning proposition."

Her heart thumped. She set her mug on the tray and sat back again, tucking her suddenly cold hands beneath the edge of the afghan.

Yes, she wanted to be independent and in control as a single mom…but she didn't want to be a single mom forever. She'd realized that truth the day she had met Michael. And even after last night's conversation and this morning's warnings to herself, she hadn't given up on him.

Until this minute.

Until his one flat statement shattered all her hopes and dreams.

Where were Callie and Lyssa to save their little sister now? She could see them shaking their heads in disbelief at hearing *this* news. She could hear them, too.

Isn't that just like poor Amber to mess things up?

Even as a four-year-old, she was always the mommy when she played house.

And now she's crushing on a man who probably runs at the first mention of marriage.

And they would be right. Michael's conviction was a

chilling reminder she couldn't trust her instincts about men. Still, couldn't she expect just one tiny Christmas miracle?

"Isn't your view of marriage a little…cynical?"

"Not in my opinion. I've seen too many folks ruined by so-called happy matrimony."

"And many more people are perfectly happy. Or can be." Even her. "Don't you ever plan to get married? And…and to have a family?"

"*Me?*" he asked, his tone incredulous. He attempted to laugh off her question, and yet his eyes were dark with something she couldn't name. "*Bah, humbug.*"

• • •

After another eardrum-rattling scream from Penny, Michael took off. He would be no help with the baby. And judging by Amber's expression after his *Bah, humbug* reply, she'd have no use for him, anyhow.

In his office on the opposite side of the living room, he paced from one end of the space to the other.

What a mess. He still hadn't found out what Amber was hiding. That story she'd spun about her mom and sisters was a crock of…*soup*.

And he'd sure dropped the ball last night. He should have told her she would have to find somewhere else to stay as of today. Instead, he had relented at the sound of despair in her voice. Despair she probably thought she had successfully hidden from him.

He heard her soft voice as she tried to soothe the baby. Penny continued to screech at regular intervals.

Colic. Chronic. Poor kid.

The cries grew louder. Amber had moved to stand near the Christmas tree. Swaying slightly, she patted the baby's back.

The twinkling lights reflected in Amber's long, silky hair. She was a head shorter than he was, slim, young, looking barely old enough to be a mom. Of course, he knew she was older than she appeared. Her resume had listed the year she finished high school. A half-dozen years after his own graduation. Not long enough to matter, but he'd grabbed onto the fact to add to his growing list of reasons to keep his distance.

The years between them put her closer to jailbait than he liked. When they'd met, the vulnerable look in her eyes tugged at him, but it also said she'd been hurt recently.

The cell phone he'd left on his desk began to ring. Out in the living room, Penny's screeches rose. Cause and effect? Who knew? But maybe stopping one noise would halt the other. He snatched up the phone. The display showed the call came from an unknown number.

"DeFranco," he said.

"Michael, my friend."

He recognized Nick Tavlock's enthusiastic voice immediately. "Hey, Nick."

"I'm calling to wish you a Merry Christmas. A *very* merry one, as a matter of fact."

For a second, he stared at the phone. He and Nick were longtime business associates. Common interests had turned them into friends. But this holiday call was a first. "Thanks. Best to you, too. You sound like you're enjoying some Christmas cheer." Thanks to Amber, he knew the reason for that.

Before he could say something about Nick and Lyssa's engagement, a noise from the living room distracted him. Penny had let out a wail.

Dead silence followed. Then Nick said, "Yeah. And you sound like you have a baby."

"It's not mine. It's Amber's—" Too late, he cut himself

off. But what difference did it make. Nick had been invited to ski parties here. He knew Amber stayed when he had guests. This trip, he didn't have anyone with him—but how would the other man know?

"Amber's there?" Nick asked. "You're at the lodge?"

"Yeah," he admitted.

"That explains why she left early, then."

"What are you talking about?" Too late again, he realized just where Nick had probably chosen to spend his Christmas. His heart sinking, he asked anyway. "Where are you?"

"In Snowflake Valley, at her folks' house," Nick said. "Amber left right after the party ended last night. Said she wasn't feeling well. Her family wondered about that. They say she gets migraines, but she wasn't complaining about any symptoms."

Penny let out another yelp. Michael would swear she'd raised the volume. He looked into the living room, but Amber had moved away from the Christmas tree and out of his view.

"Hold on a minute," Nick said.

"Nick, wait—" Too late yet again. Maybe that third time had been the charm, he'd gotten lucky, and the call had dropped. Cell service at this elevation could be unreliable, especially in bad weather. But the murmur of voices in his ear said his luck had run out. Nick had only put the phone down to talk to someone else.

Penny's screech grew a few decibels louder. He covered the phone with his hand.

Amber appeared in the doorway with the baby resting against her shoulder. "Did you just say *Nick*?" she asked.

Great. Over all the noise, she'd still managed to hear that. He nodded.

"Hey, Michael," Nick said in his ear.

"Amber's fine," he said tightly, hoping to cut the conversation short. Her jaw dropped in surprise.

"I'm sure Lyssa will be happy to hear it. But that's not why I called. It's a lucky break, finding you here in Snowflake Valley." *Lucky for you, maybe.* "I wanted to talk to you, anyhow, and face-to-face is much better. You're not going anywhere in the next hour, are you?"

"Where would I go? It's Christmas." He was spending the holiday with a colicky baby and—judging by Amber's expression now—that baby's very cranky mom.

"Great," Nick said. "See you soon."

The phone went silent. Not meeting Amber's eyes, Michael ended the call. He set the cell carefully on the edge of the desk again.

"Nick *Tavlock*?" she asked.

He nodded.

"*Where would I go?*" she repeated in dismay.

He winced. "Yeah. Nick and Lyssa are on their way up from the valley."

"You told him I was here?"

"No. Not directly. Technically, Penny told him. Nick heard her when she yelled—"

"And then you told Nick who she was."

"Yeah. Sorry. Guess the secret's out."

"*Michael*," she screeched, sounding just like her daughter.

Chapter Three

Cuddling Penny close to her, Amber set the rocking chair near the kitchen window into motion again. She had told Michael she needed to rock Penny to soothe her colic. Which was perfectly true.

Okay, so maybe she hadn't added her other reason for fleeing his office—being one breath away from having a meltdown like a snowman in July, right there in front of him. This new twist to her predicament wasn't his fault. Much. And though she didn't want to admit it, Michael had told her the truth, too.

The secret's out.

"And you notice," she told Penny, "he hasn't made an appearance since."

Ice crystals pinged against the window. That figured. "The weather's terrible. The roads will be treacherous. And thanks to your mommy, Aunt Lyssa's due here any minute." After racing up the mountainside with her new fiancé, she would most likely arrive armed with the idea of coming to her sister's rescue.

The doorbell rang. *Oh, joy.*

Groaning, she held Penny closer to her. Cuddling as they rocked usually helped to calm her as much as it soothed the baby. Not today.

Lyssa appeared in the doorway. "Well! What a surprise to find out you were here. Why didn't you tell us you were driving up to the lodge this morning?"

"Merry Christmas to you, too," Amber said dryly. "That ought to be obvious, considering your reaction right now. And how quickly *you* got here this morning." No need to mention she and Penny had come here straight from the party last night.

"Oh, no. That's on Nick. He wants to talk to Michael. And do you mean you didn't say anything about going to the lodge because we'd be concerned about you?"

"No. I didn't say anything because you're all worried I can't take care of myself. And Penny."

Lyssa laughed. "That's ridiculous. You're a great mom. Everybody in Snowflake Valley knows that. But yes, if I'd known, I would have worried about you driving up here in the storm. And yes, I'd have called to make sure you and Penny arrived okay. Just as I would for anyone else in the family." She took the seat at the table closest to the rocking chair. "I knew something was up," she said in a lower voice. "Nobody misses Mom's cinnamon rolls on Christmas morning. There's something going on between you and Michael, isn't there?"

What? "No, there—"

"Amber," Lyssa interrupted, grinning. "You know better than to lie on Christmas Day. Santa will come back and demand you return every one of your presents." She crossed her arms on the table. "You might as well tell me. I'm not getting out of this seat until you do."

Amber sighed. "We're not in grade school, Lys, and trading secrets." Bad example. Maybe Lyssa hadn't noticed her cringe.

"You're right. We're all grown up now and able to talk about the opposite sex without breaking into giggles."

Her big sister thought this was all about *Michael.* If only…

"Now, tell me what's going on with you two."

"Nothing's going on."

"Then that's a real shame, considering you're here alone with him. At least, when Nick and I arrived, I didn't see anyone else out there in the living room." Dropping her teasing tone, she added, "Come on, Amber. You know you can talk to me."

She did know. But she had nothing to say about Michael. And she didn't want to discuss what had really brought her to the lodge. They needed to change topics before she cracked under the pressure.

Thankfully, the sound of footsteps and deep voices growing louder announced Michael and Nick's approach to the kitchen. Lyssa shot her a frustrated glance, then looked expectantly at the doorway. Amber managed a smile just as the two men entered.

"Hey, Amber," Nick said. "Michael's singing your praises for helping him out, especially on a holiday."

Helping him out? Exactly what had he said? She didn't dare open her mouth or even look at him. Instead, she fixed her smile in place, stared in his general direction, and held her breath.

He took a seat at the table and turned to Lyssa. "Yeah, I decided at the last minute to spend a few days here. Amber was nice enough to have the heat turned up for me when I arrived. She's about to scramble eggs for breakfast. Can we interest you in some? And we have plenty of coffee. Don't we, Amber?"

She started. "Of course. I'll put another pot on and get going on breakfast." After settling the baby in her playpen, she crossed the kitchen to the coffeemaker. She was glad for the chance to get away from the group at the table. To try to get a handle on the situation.

Why would Michael go to these lengths to help her?

He hadn't actually lied outright. She *had* turned the heat up before he had arrived. And she *had* offered to make eggs. When it came to the details, though, he was skating on thin ice. And in Snowflake Valley, that was a very dangerous place to be.

• • •

While Amber scrambled the eggs, Lyssa helped her with the coffee. At the table with Nick, Michael could see the other man had something on his mind.

Sure enough, as soon as they were all seated, Nick turned to him. "You were so busy talking about Amber, you never asked what brought us all the way up the mountain on Christmas morning."

Right. Because he'd been a breath away from telling his buddy he ought to reconsider the whole marriage idea.

Amber had taken the seat beside him. As if she'd heard the thought, she tightened her fingers on her mug.

Thanks to her, Michael knew what was coming. But he couldn't resist prolonging the inevitable. "Well, let's see. You didn't bring skis. And you haven't mentioned settling in with a movie and some popcorn. I'm guessing sooner or later you'll offer an explanation."

"Not an explanation. An announcement." Nick wrapped his arm around Lyssa, seated beside him. "We're getting married."

"Hey, great news. Congratulations." He reached across the table to shake Nick's free hand. Even Amber wouldn't be able to find fault with his enthusiastic response.

A quick glance showed him she might not have noticed.

She sat staring down into her mug as if she had hopes of reading the future in it. Or as if she were seeing the past and remembering what he had told her about matrimony.

It wasn't a winning proposition.

At least, not in his experience. But he wouldn't say that to the prospective bride and groom, who now wore matching smiles. "When's the big day?"

"We haven't set a date yet," Lyssa said.

"When we do, you'll be the first to know," Nick told him. "I'm counting on you to be my best man."

His hand jerked reflexively, almost spilling his coffee.

Great. Just what he needed—to get all decked out in a penguin suit to participate in an event he didn't believe in. The things you did for people because they were your friends. The things you would do for your family, if you didn't have one like his.

"Sounds like we've got a lot to celebrate," he said. "You both should join us for dinner, on me, if you're around later in the week."

"That works," Nick said. "Unless Lyssa has the calendar filled." Spoken like a devoted husband already. Another good man lost.

"We'll make the time," she said brightly. "Thanks for the invitation. Believe me, this is one dinner I wouldn't miss for the world."

"To tell the truth," Nick said, "when I called, I was surprised to find you were here. I'd have thought you'd be spending the day with your family. Don't you usually?"

Michael took a sip of coffee and set the mug on the kitchen table. Earlier, his cups from the first pot had tasted just fine. More likely it was the other man's question about family that had left a bitter taste in his mouth. "No, we're not always together for Christmas."

"That's sad," Amber said in a flat tone, just like when

she'd called him Scrooge.

"What's sad about it?" he asked. "I'm taking advantage of the chance for rest and relaxation. Speaking of which..." He turned to his buddy. "You'll have to come back up again for a day on the slopes while I'm still here. Both of you." If Lyssa could fit it into their schedule.

"Sounds good to me," Nick said.

Lyssa nodded. "You didn't mention having any other guests with you on this trip. Are you here all alone?"

Amber's mug tilted, sloshing coffee over the rim. She grabbed for her napkin.

"All alone," he echoed.

"I'm sorry, but I agree with Amber," Lyssa said. "Families should be together for Christmas. Don't you think so, Nick?"

His friend smiled. "That's one loaded question. And yes, you know I think so." He turned to Michael. "I'm glad you're sticking around for a while. You can help me hold out against the rest of the Barnetts."

"Oh, stop." Laughing, Lyssa shook her head.

"Hold out against what?" Michael asked.

"They're trying to get me involved in one of their family fundraising projects."

"Well, then, yeah. Count on my help. I'd draw the line at that, too."

Amber looked up. Her smile seemed forced, but at least now he had the pleasure of eye contact with her. "That's not an option for Nick," she said. "Not since he's marrying into *this* family. We're talking about Snowflake Valley's annual Winter Festival. Barnetts have been in charge of running it since the town began."

"And this year's festival will be even more special," Lyssa said. "Michael, you remember our sister, Callie?"

He nodded. One day last winter, his ski party had come across Amber with Lyssa and Callie at the local diner, the

Candy Cane.

Who in the world would call a diner that? The entire town was filled with businesses with quaint, quirky names—which could explain why he didn't often venture down the mountain when he came here. He liked the lodge being out of the way. Secluded. Peaceful. But given how he felt about Christmas, he was beginning to wonder why he'd ever bought property in a place called Snowflake Valley.

"Callie's a teacher," Lyssa reminded him. "She volunteered all of us to help her organize a fundraiser for the elementary school."

"Ah. I see your problem," he said soberly to Nick.

"Yeah. But I'm working on a way to take a pass."

Amber and Lyssa both shouted his name at once. Served the man right for getting himself trapped into an engagement. Grinning, he waited to see whether or not Nick would get himself out this conversation alive.

Instead, to his surprise, Lyssa laughed. "Oh, but that's not the only volunteer project Callie has on her mind. Amber, she's nominating you for Snow Ball Queen."

"*No.*" Amber's fork clattered onto her plate.

Michael frowned,

"What's that?" Nick asked.

"Tomorrow is the kickoff of the week-long festival," Lyssa said. "The Snow Ball is the grand finale."

Nick nodded. "That's the dance you told me about. The one at the community center on New Year's Eve."

"Right. Everyone in Snowflake Valley votes for King and Queen of the Snow Ball. The winners are announced that night."

Nick frowned. "No offense to Amber, but why isn't Callie nominating you, too?"

"Thanks." Lyssa kissed his cheek. "But she can't. I'm not eligible to compete."

"Eligible?" Nick echoed.

Let him be the front man here. Michael settled back in his chair and sipped his coffee. This deal sounded worse than the Barnetts' family project. No way would he get involved in either one.

"I'm not eligible since I'm attached," Lyssa explained. "Everybody in town knows that when someone competes for Snow Ball King or Queen, they're declaring themselves single and looking."

Amber's face turned as pale as her white ceramic mug, as if whatever illness bypassed her last night had just hit full-force. "I refuse to run."

"You know the rules as well as I do. If someone is nominated, their name goes on the ballot."

"I won't participate."

He caught it again—that same hint of despair he'd heard in her voice last night. Maybe this snowball thing tied into the secret she was keeping from her family.

"Hmm…" Lyssa shrugged. "Well, it's true you don't have to *pursue* winning the crown. But how will it look for Mom and Dad if a Barnett is nominated but doesn't make even an attempt to win?"

"I can't…"

"Why not?" Lyssa demanded.

"Because…because…" Amber's gaze met his. He didn't read anything close to a plea for help in those blue eyes, couldn't find the hint of a silent SOS. Of course not. Amber's independent streak would never let her lean on him. Yet he still felt the need to give her an out—maybe since he could relate to having family push her against the wall.

What the heck… He reached for her hand. "Amber can't compete," he said firmly, "because we're together."

Her fingers clamped around his, nearly cutting off his circulation.

Lyssa's jaw dropped.

Nick slapped him on the shoulder.

Amber stared at him, her eyes now like twin blue pools, as the saying went. Eyes he could drown in—if she didn't kill him first.

Chapter Four

"Michael, what were you *thinking*?" Amber clutched the dishtowel in both fists. Then she swallowed a near-hysterical laugh.

Just look at her—one step away from wringing her hands like some cartoon damsel in distress.

As if he thought she might fall apart before his eyes, Michael headed across the room toward her. "Deep breath, Amber."

"*Deep* breath? I'm lucky I can breathe at all." *Partly because you're two feet away from me.* She dropped the towel on the counter. "Do you know what you've done?"

"Yeah. Gotten you off the hook for that thing Lyssa talked about. You looked two seconds away from a panic attack."

So much for believing she'd appeared calm and rational while working out the perfect rebuttals for her sister's arguments. Why did Michael have to see the truth? Why did he have to make everything worse?

She refused to think about the little thrill running

through her at knowing he'd come to her rescue. "What does it matter how I looked? Now you've gotten Lyssa stuck on another track. The one about us being a couple."

"I'm not sure she actually fell for that story."

She rolled her eyes. Poor man. "You saw her. Nick could barely get her out the door. I had to promise you'd be coming along to my parents' house for dinner." At that reminder, he had the grace to look ashamed about his lie. Or maybe uncomfortable, as if reality had hit him squarely between the eyes. Those beautiful dark eyes.

Go away, Michael. Don't look so good, so mouthwateringly tempting. Don't stand right here when you're so far out of my reach.

Hands shaking, she turned and began putting their breakfast dishes in the dishwasher. Work would keep her mind off Michael. Yeah, and on this Christmas morning snowmen would fly.

Lyssa had wanted to help clear up, but Amber had insisted she could handle it. It was everything else she couldn't manage. Hearing about the Snow Ball Queen nomination had been bad enough. But now, having Michael say they were together?

So much for not thinking of him. "Oh, Lyssa believed you, all right. *You* just won't believe what you're in for."

"Such as?"

"My family is big on togetherness. And when there's someone...important in any of our lives, that someone becomes part of the family." That was an understatement... her family took in those someones as though they were long-lost relatives. "We're doomed."

He laughed. "Hey. No worries." He touched her arm. She started, nearly losing her grip on a dinner plate. "We'll put on a good show."

She almost gave herself whiplash turning to stare at him.

"What kind of show?"

"We'll pretend we're a couple. As long as you don't jump every time I come near you, the way you did just now, we'll be fine."

That little jump was nothing compared to the happy-dance going on inside her. What a fool. Yet, already visions sweeter than sugarplums were scrolling through her mind, scenes of her holiday afternoon filled with gifts. Michael's hand in hers. Michael's arm around her waist. Michael holding her close as—

"I'm sure we'll manage to get through one dinner."

What? She blinked. "One dinner? You think that's all it will be?" She gestured with the plate she held. "That's about as likely as my making this sail across the room."

"No throwing the dishes. I get enough of that at my dad's house. What's the big deal? So, it's one afternoon. We'll handle it."

"You've already talked to Lyssa and Nick about dinner out and skiing."

He shrugged. "All right, that makes sense. Nick's my best friend. As Lyssa put it, I'd make time for those things. Other than that, just tell everyone I need to hole up here at the lodge because I've got a lot of work to do. Which I have."

All traces of amusement vanished. He suddenly looked grim. Abruptly, he returned to the table. What had changed his mood so quickly?

"Besides," he added, "I'm only here for a week."

Talk about grim. One short week… When would she see him again? And why did she care? Despite his whopper of a white lie, they weren't "together."

"You're here at the busiest time of year in Snowflake Valley," she explained. "And my family is involved in *everything*. Where I go, they'll expect you to go. Just like Lyssa and Nick. He's only here through New Year's, too."

He shrugged. "You'll figure out something to tell them when I'm not around."

"*Me?*"

"Yeah. As you said, they're your family. When you get right down to it, if you hadn't been staying here, none of this could have happened. And now that we're on the subject…" He paused. Her fingers locked onto a handful of silverware. The silence went on so long, she could hear Penny's soft cooing from the playpen. Finally, he said, "You owe me, Amber."

"What? How do you figure that?"

"I did you a favor and got you out of that ball. Besides, I'm your boss and this is my lodge. Now tell me why you moved in here."

She stared at him, her mind racing. He stared back at her, unblinking. Did he hope a mind-meld would make her reveal the truth? Lots of luck with that.

But another long silence did the job for him, pushing her into speech. "You said you didn't mind if I stayed here."

"I don't."

"You said yourself it was better to have the lodge occupied some of the time."

"It is."

"Then what does it matter why I'm here?" Even as she asked the question, she knew it did matter. She was stalling, only because she didn't want to tell Michael what had really brought her to the lodge.

Sighing, she dropped the silverware into the caddy and closed the dishwasher door. "I told you, I need a place to stay for a few days."

"And you didn't want to ask your family."

"Right." His steady gaze told her he wouldn't let this go. "They…love me."

He raised his eyebrows. "And that's the problem?"

"Yes. Well, part of it." The biggest part. But how could she explain that to him? "Until my younger sisters and brothers were born, I was always Lyssa and Callie's baby sister. The one they had to save." She flushed. "They talked me out of stage fright before my kindergarten graduation ceremony. Tutored me through every grade of elementary school math. Rescued me from schoolyard bullies."

"And you relied on them."

She grimaced. "Yes, I relied on them. I was too young to know any better. But even now, even when I don't ask for help, they come to my rescue." Just the memories of those times made her more determined to be independent.

"But you want to stand on your own."

She stared. "Hey, who's telling this story, anyhow?" Her laugh sounded shaky.

"You are. And you're getting to the part where you tell me why you're here."

The laughter died in her throat. Suddenly needing support, she rested one hip against the kitchen island. Avoiding his eyes, she smoothed the edges of the woven placemats she had stacked there. "The plain and simple truth is, the electricity in my apartment was turned off."

"Because…"

No, he wouldn't quit until she had confessed all. "Because I couldn't pay my bill."

"That doesn't happen to first-time offenders."

She flinched. He thought she was a criminal? Or maybe she was being too sensitive. She raised her chin and met his gaze. "It wasn't the first time," she admitted. "But the other times, I was able to make payments in the grace period, and they never shut off the service."

"What happened this time?"

His suddenly softer tone made her wince. She didn't want pity. But maybe she was overreacting again. It wasn't like she didn't hear questions from anyone else. Her family had plenty of them, too, especially when she got herself caught in a dilemma and they wanted to help her out.

Except maybe her instincts *were* on-target. Maybe *his* concern came from something more—from the thought she wasn't an employee he could trust. "I didn't do anything wrong. I just loaned some money to a friend, and he hasn't paid me back."

"*He?*"

Unknowingly, Michael had jumped on the last point she wanted to discuss—the fact she had let another man take advantage of her. "Yes, *he*. Man, woman…that definitely doesn't matter. He's a friend, and he needed the money for his family. How could I refuse, especially when it's Christmastime?"

"How could you have given him a loan," he countered, "when you had bills of your own to pay?"

"I would have been able to handle the bills…if he had paid me back on time. He promised he would return the money before the holidays."

"According to my calendar, those days have come and gone."

"Yes, I know. And here it is, Christmas Day. You don't need to remind me. He'll pay me back. When he can."

"You took his word on trust?"

He'd asked the question mildly, but still, she cringed. It was exactly what her family would have pointed out to her. Especially Callie and Lyssa.

You're too softhearted, Amber.

You need to look out for yourself, not worry about everyone else.

And of course, she agreed with them, especially now that she had Penny to care for. Still, she also had a heart, even if it got her into trouble—something Michael didn't need to know. "I prefer to think of what I did as giving a friend the benefit of the doubt."

"Meanwhile, what are you going to do?"

She shrugged and forced herself to say lightly, "Hold out hope for peace on Earth and goodwill from my fellow man."

"Including your employer?"

He hadn't gotten the sarcasm. She didn't want help from anyone. And yet, relief rushed through her. "Are you offering goodwill?" She would never take a loan from Michael, not after the admissions she had just made. But he *was* her boss. And at this point, to keep her family in the dark about her situation, she would gratefully accept the same Christmas bonus he probably gave to all his employees.

He smiled. "There's already something extra coming in your next direct deposit. And, of course, you're welcome to stay here until you get things straightened out."

"Thank you," she said, truly grateful for the additional pay...and much happier than she should have been about her chance to be with him.

"The lodge is definitely big enough," he went on. "We'll go our separate ways."

"After Christmas dinner with my family."

"After Christmas dinner," he agreed. "Except for meals here, too, we shouldn't run into each other at all. And I'll have the solitude I came looking for...to get some work done." Again, that grim expression crossed his face.

There went her happiness factor, too.

Maybe she should have mentioned the quiet she'd promised didn't come with a guarantee.

• • •

True to her word, Amber had left him alone for the rest of the morning. Between their late breakfast with Nick and Lyssa and the upcoming Christmas dinner at her folks' house, they had agreed to skip lunch. Once or twice, he had wandered into the kitchen to grab a cup of coffee. He didn't see any sign of her or the baby.

Not that he'd been looking.

By the time he had arrived in Snowflake Valley last night, it had been too late to get to the store. Normally, he'd have emailed Amber and asked her to pick up whatever groceries he'd need. But this time he hadn't come with guests. And he'd somehow managed to keep from reneging on his agreement with himself, the one that said he wouldn't see her at all this trip.

So much for that plan.

He had spent the hours in his office trying not to think about her. *Wanting* not to think about her. Not much luck with that, either. What a fool. He had plenty of ways to distract himself. To keep busy. He glared at the equipment spread out on his desk.

"Ooh, watch out, Michael." Her voice rang out from the office doorway. "Your face might freeze that way. Right, Penny?"

He grabbed the tilting, not-quite-empty coffee mug before it could hit his laptop.

"Sorry," she said in a much quieter voice. "I didn't mean to startle you."

Served him right for getting so wrapped up in thoughts of her. The vision in the doorway looked even better than the one in his mind. Amber held a bundle it wouldn't take a genius to know was her blanket-wrapped baby. Above the bundle, her blue eyes sparkled. Her cheeks were pink, probably since she already wore her heavy knitted jacket. A red woolen hat made her hair look more gold than brown.

Why had he ever thought Snowflake Valley would be the perfect place to escape from his family? Would he have come to the lodge if he'd known he would find Amber and Penny here?

"Did any of your coffee spill?" she asked.

"No. I might have been better off if it had. Sometimes frying all this equipment seems like the best thing for it."

She laughed. "That's a heck of an attitude, considering you own an electronics company."

"Do I? Or does it own me? I have no idea what you've been up to all morning." *Great. Why not just come out and tell her you missed her?* Quickly, he gestured at the desktop. "But I've been chained to the desk here. Checking preliminary year-end sales reports. Reviewing profit-and-loss statements. Shuffling all the other paperwork that goes along with owning a business—even if that paper's mostly electronic now, too." Either way, it was work he would gladly have done without.

Same for the holidays. He *had* tried telling that to Amber, and she had called him Scrooge. He could handle that. But he hated this time of year, both for all the administrative headaches he had to deal with and for the stress hangovers he had to fight after the battles at his family's get-togethers.

"But you're the boss," she said. "You should have people doing all that for you."

"Try telling that to my accountant." He laughed shortly. "Actually, it is part of my job. CEO's get some perks, including the right to delegate, but they don't get to pass the buck completely."

"I thought you loved your job. You always said you did."

"Good memory."

Too good. It went along with everything else...good about her.

Whenever he'd brought associates to the lodge, Amber had stayed on-site to cook for him and his guests. Seems like those business meetings had occurred more and more often as the year went on. He'd told himself dissatisfaction over the job drove him here. But lately, he'd begun to question that.

In all his conversations with Amber, he had gotten to know her, probably better than he should have. He'd run off at the mouth too much then, too. But she'd been easy to talk to, open, sincere, fun. And though she probably didn't know it, her face usually gave away her emotions.

Like the concern he was seeing there now. Maybe that's what prodded him to go on. "I did love the job. Once." He had thought it would fill his life. And it did, just not the way he'd planned. "I didn't think I'd get reduced to this much of a paper-pusher," he added.

And that's all he'd say. Not the part about being bored. Or feeling disillusioned. And definitely not the part about his fear. The fear that ate at him on a daily basis. The understanding that if he didn't have the work he loved, he had nothing.

He nudged the laptop closed and grabbed his cell phone. "You two ready to go?"

Nodding, she adjusted Penny's blanket. "I can't wait. I'm hungry for a big turkey dinner and all the trimmings, plus dessert. What could be better?" No mention of the roles they would have to play. Before he could remind her, she added, "And please don't say *Bah, humbug* again. Those are all things that make Christmas so special."

"Not *my* Christmas."

Dang. Too late to swallow those words. Thinking about his own family, his job, his lack of interest in the work... that's all he'd needed to prime his irritation. At himself. But he'd taken the feeling out on Amber. Because in spite of her glowing expression, her talk of Christmas had triggered something dark inside him—the knowledge that he had no memories of ever celebrating a holiday the way she had.

Take this year's aborted attempt, for example. He never

should have gone to his dad's house.

He never should have agreed to let Amber stay here.

She shook her head. Here it came, the blasting he deserved for snapping at her.

"Well," she said softly, "why don't we change things up? We'll make today your chance to see what a real Christmas is like."

Chapter Five

Amber stole a glance at Michael in the driver's seat of his SUV. This morning, she had wondered why the mention of work made him look so grim. Now she knew. It hurt her heart to know he didn't love his job the way she loved hers. Or that…

Oh, don't go there. Bad enough that in just minutes she would have to pretend to be "together" with Michael. She couldn't let anyone see how she really felt about him.

This could turn out to be the worst week of her life. Or the best—if you believed in miracles.

After pulling onto the street she indicated, he said, "We probably should have prepped."

"For *Christmas*?"

His laugh seemed to fill the enclosed space. It definitely filled her heart with joy.

Don't go there, either.

"No, not for Christmas. For the afternoon we need to get through."

She blinked. So much for joy. And what about the big

plan to have Scrooge enjoy the holiday? Hopefully, the jury was still out on that one. "Turn here. This is it."

He pulled up close to the snow-swept front steps of her family home and came around to help her out of the SUV. When he took her arm, her startled breath of surprise misted in the cold air. A dead giveaway. A visual reminder to watch her reactions today.

As she moved to the rear seat to get Penny, he asked, "How many are there in your family?"

"Ten, counting my parents and the baby. You've met Callie and Lyssa. They're the two oldest, then me. After us, we have a set of twin sisters and two younger brothers."

He looked up at the house she had lived in until a short time ago. "Big place. You and the others are out on your own?"

"No, actually, they all still live at home."

His eyes widened, as if her answer had surprised him. "You're the only who's left the nest permanently?"

"So far. The twins are in college, but of course they come back on their breaks." Unlike Michael, as he had told her. Or if he did go home, it wasn't willingly. How sad, again. No wonder the man didn't like Christmas.

"What makes you so independent?" he asked.

She hesitated, fiddling with Penny's blanket. What could she say? Definitely not that after her ex had left she had been too full of wounded pride—and too ashamed of her mistake in marrying him—to go back home. And positively not that Michael had been her hero, stepping in with his job offer at the point she had needed it most. "I just…like living on my own. With Penny."

"Yeah. Amber…" He paused, looking down at her, then reached out to trace her cheek with one finger. A cold and padded finger, covered by his glove. And still she felt the warmth of him. Or thought she did. He smiled. "Just testing to make sure you wouldn't jump. Doing this job right is going to involve us getting close. And probably some touching."

Getting close and *touching* sounded so good. So right. But the word that stood out to her was *job*.

"No worries, boss." There she went again, lying on Christmas Day. But what choice did she have? "Anything you can dish out, I can handle."

He laughed. "Good to know." Backing up a step, he looked at the house again. "The porch has been swept, too. You and the baby get in out of the cold. I'll go park this thing."

She nodded. As she reached the top of the steps, the SUV eased away.

"What a Christmas this is going to be," she said to Penny. "Spending the day here with Grandma and Grandpa and everybody, pretending I'm actually dating my boss. And then going back home… I mean, going back *to the lodge* to spend Christmas night with Scrooge." More than that, she and Penny would spend days living with a man who didn't like crying babies and wanted to be left alone. Not the best omens for their temporary living arrangement.

She refused to even think about Michael's attitude toward marriage.

"Luckily," she told Penny, "he's right. It's a big lodge. We'll just make sure to stay out of Scrooge's way and not bother him."

As if showing she could hold up her end of the bargain, Penny gazed up at her without making a sound.

From her parents' living room, Amber could smell the rich scent of turkey roasting in the kitchen. The tree lights and electric candlesticks on the fireplace mantel were lit. Piles of wrapped packages covered the floor around the tree. The thought of Michael never having special holiday memories like these made her heart hurt again.

Her dad appeared in the hallway. "Merry Christmas!" he called.

"Merry Christmas to you, too."

"About time you got here."

She started, then covered the response by setting Penny in her carrier on the couch. "Why? Was Mom or someone trying to reach me? I have the cell phone on." Read that as: Did they try the apartment phone last night and not get an answer? But no...if that had happened, Lyssa would have mentioned it.

"Not that I know of," Dad said. "I just want to see my granddaughter."

"Oh, and not your daughter?"

"I have four more of those." Laughing, he tugged on her hat. "You know I love you, hon, but I've got only one grandbaby—so far."

She smiled. If Dad had long ago gotten his way, he would have a handful of grandkids by now. He unbuckled the straps of the carrier and lifted Penny to cuddle her against his chest.

He wrapped his free arm around Amber. Her eyes misting, she rested her head against his shoulder. Just for a moment, she wanted to go back to the days when her dad's hug could make everything better. But those days were over. And she could never regret growing up and learning to face some challenges on her own, especially now that she had her daughter.

"I heard the good news about you and Michael," he went on. "Maybe one of these days, Penny will have a new brother or sister."

Flushing, she unzipped her jacket.

Forget asking Michael what *he* had been thinking this morning. How had *she* ever let him talk her into his crazy idea, into believing they could get away with pretending they were dating? Or…could it be? Had she wanted to believe this was the real thing?

At this rate, it would be better if Michael didn't find a parking spot until he reached the California border. "Dad, please don't go on like that when Michael comes in. The news is…nice. But it's very *new* news." *To us all.* "You'd better start expanding your search for prospective moms. Since the twins are too young to give you any grandkids yet, I recommend you have this chat with Callie. And definitely with Lyssa, now that she's engaged."

"Are you talking about me again?"

Amber turned to find her sister leaning against the stairway railing. Although from a distance some folks in Snowflake Valley couldn't tell the three oldest Barnett sisters apart, Lyssa had the darkest brown hair, inherited from their dad. She made a show of fluffing her curls and giving Amber an exaggerated smirk.

Amber laughed. "Talking about you *again?* Don't you mean *still*? Since the party last night, Penny and I haven't discussed anything but your engagement."

If she didn't count Scrooge.

Stop thinking about Michael. Stop thinking about men, period. Making one ginormous mistake in trying to find a forever relationship ought to be enough for anyone. But getting involved with Michael would be worse, times ten. He was her boss. The provider of her paycheck. The man who would give her a dream that *could* come true—not a life with him, but a home for her and Penny.

She and her daughter were a team. They didn't need anyone else.

As Dad took Penny down the hallway to the kitchen, Lyssa approached, waggling her fingers to show off her temporary engagement ring. Sadly, Amber recalled the beautiful ring their older sister Callie had once worn. She tried not to think of the diamond solitaire she had once hoped for but had never gotten. With most of their money going toward the apartment, they'd barely had enough left to buy wedding bands. A good thing, after all. For her and Penny, a place to live was so much more important than a mocking reminder of a bad marriage.

Amber squinted at Lyssa and pretended to shield her eyes from a blazing light. "Put that rock away, or I won't be able to see to eat my dinner. And why are you all alone? Where's your brand-new better half?"

"Upstairs. And yours?"

"Parking," she said shortly, eyeing the calculating look Lyssa gave her. Maybe Michael had been right after all. Who would have thought it? But maybe her next-older sister hadn't completely bought their story, after all.

"Are you okay?" Lyssa asked.

She jumped. "I'm fine. Why?"

"You seem distracted. Not yourself."

For a second, she felt tempted to confess everything. To blurt out the truth and ask for help. She could trust both Lyssa and Callie to come to her aid. But just as she had told Michael, relying on them was part of her problem. She couldn't let her family know what she had gotten herself into now. They'd never leave her alone again.

"I'm fine," she assured Lyssa. "I was thinking I need to go wish Mom a Merry Christmas. And we should see if she needs any help getting dinner ready."

"Right," her sister said dryly. "As if you really expect me to fall for that. The truth is, you're just hoping to swipe a leftover cinnamon roll from breakfast."

"Busted." She forced a laugh. "Well, we can't call it Christmas without a few cinnamon rolls." Or without a big turkey dinner, special desserts, and gifts. And without joy and laughter and family and friends.

Her eyes suddenly misting again, she thought of a snow-covered mountainside and of a man on his own inside a secluded ski lodge.

No matter what she would have to suffer through today—Dad's teasing, Lyssa's questions, Michael's nearness and his touch—*oh, yes, please, his touch…* No matter any of those things, she was glad she hadn't left that man all alone on Christmas Day.

• • •

Considering Amber's fears of how her family would behave, Michael found the Barnetts a low-key bunch. Especially compared to what he had to grow up with.

Mrs. Barnett had stopped supervising the dinner prep long enough to pause beside him. Her brown curls were graying around the edges. Still, she looked nearly as young as her three eldest daughters, who strongly resembled her. She'd given him a big smile. "Hello, Michael. We're very glad you're here." Then she'd hurried off, leaving him feeling more pleased than that simple welcome had warranted.

He had gone through a few interesting moments fielding straightforward questions from Mr. Barnett. The man was tall and thin with dark hair that, like his wife's, had grayed around the edges. They both could probably blame that on raising a houseful of kids.

When the man's questions veered toward his business, he had felt Amber's gaze on him. He'd said too much to her about his job. She was his employee, not his best friend. But he'd always found her a good listener.

"Well," Mr. Barnett said, "let's get the introductions over with and then settle in at the table."

Michael earned a few giggles from the red-haired girl twins and received a couple of "hey, mans" and handshakes from the teenaged boys. Callie and Lyssa, the two oldest, he had met before. And Nick, of course, who looked right at home as they took seats at the crowded dining room table. Very crowded.

No problem. The tight space put him closer to Amber. So far, between helping to set the table and carrying dishes from the kitchen, she'd had very little to say. Very little to do with him, come to think of it. He was in this for her, wasn't he? The least she could do was pay him some attention. He shifted his chair even closer, letting his arm graze hers.

For a moment, she froze. Then she turned, smiling, to hand him a bowl. The pleasure of that smile was worth the risk of touching her. But to his dismay, he found himself wanting more from her than a dish of cranberries.

"Have you decided yet if you're going to fight the boys for a drumstick?" she asked.

He tried not to frown. In his house, arguments at dinnertime were the main course. "I'll pass on that, seeing as I'm only a guest."

"Oh, no you're not," Lyssa said. "Any friend of a Barnett is like one of the family."

Amber hadn't been kidding about that, after all. He should have taken notes on everything else she'd said.

Callie leaned forward. "Now Dad's done carving, we really need to get down to business." Her eyes gleamed with the same passion for organizing he frequently saw in his office manager's expression.

"We're having a committee meeting?" one of the boys asked. "But it's Christmas."

"And tomorrow's lunch, then the festival kickoff, and the next day we need to start getting everything ready for the auction. And," she said, "Nick and Michael need to be brought up to speed on our discussions."

"I'm good, thanks," Nick said. Lyssa elbowed him, and

he laughed and wrapped his arm around her. "Only kidding."

Michael said nothing, just took each dish handed to him and spooned food onto his plate. Sweet potatoes. Stuffing. Green-bean casserole. Corn. Gravy. A biscuit—okay, two. Much more interesting than the topic on the table. Let the Barnetts discuss anything they wanted. He had no intention of getting wrapped up in the family projects.

"This committee meeting is in honor of the Winter Festival?" Nick asked. The poor guy must have accepted he had no choice but to go along.

"Not really," Callie said. "Mom and Dad have co-chaired the festival since they took over from our grandparents. We can all do our jobs for that blindfolded. What we need to talk about now is the silent auction."

"Callie thought of having a fundraiser to help her school," Mrs. Barnett said proudly. "And the silent auction was all Amber's idea." She sent each of those daughters a smile.

"It wasn't *all* mine, Mom," Amber protested. "Callie and I did some brainstorming together."

"We did," Callie agreed. "I had a lot of great help in the initial stages. And I'm going to need a lot more now."

"That's what we're here for," Lyssa said.

"We" *does not include me.* He was not becoming part of this group.

"Callie's announcing the auction at the start of the festival tomorrow," Amber explained to Nick. Considering she had come up with the idea, she seemed oddly content to give her sister all the credit. "We're going to store the donated items in her classroom at the school, while the kids are still on their winter break."

"And that's why we're having the auction the same week as the festival," Lyssa said with a laugh. "The teachers are on break, too, so they can help out."

"Yes," Callie said, "but we're running into problems.

Some of them scheduled out-of-town family visits. And I've had a few call to tell me they're down with the flu. That's why I need you all to pitch in."

"Do we get paid?" one of the twins asked.

"Very funny." Callie wasn't smiling.

The other twin leaned forward. "What do you need us to do?"

Callie held up one hand, and again he recognized the passion for organization. Did Amber ever have the chance to run anything? Or did her oldest sister always take over? No wonder she felt so strongly about standing on her own two feet.

Callie began counting off on her fingers. "We need to make posters and flyers and bidding slips for the auction. We'll need teams to pick up the donations and store them in my room. Then, later, to transfer them to the community center. And at the end of the auction, we'll have to rearrange the room to set up for the Snow Ball."

The ball that, thanks to Callie, had brought him to this table today. Beside him, Amber froze. Maybe she was remembering how close she'd come to being nominated.

"And of course," Callie added, "we'll also need to go through the bids to pick the winners."

"And that's just for starters," Lyssa said.

One of the boys groaned.

"It's not as bad as it sounds," Amber said in a soothing tone.

This time she glanced at him and offered a smile. It was enough to get him ready to volunteer his services to her…but for something much better than her family's pet projects.

Not a thought he should have. Not a place he should go. One look around this table proved that.

Amber was definitely a home-and-family kind of woman. And he'd never be anything but a bachelor, a man on his own.

Chapter Six

After dinner and the gift exchange, Amber eagerly rose from her seat in the living room. She loved the next event on the Barnetts' annual agenda. Caroling on Christmas night was one of her favorite parts of the holiday. This year would be even more special with Michael here.

"Follow us," she told him.

At the front entry, Josh already stood by the hall closet with Drew next to him. "The line forms to the right," Josh announced. "You know the drill."

"Nick and Michael don't," Brooke protested.

"First time for everything," Nick said. "Right, Michael?"

"Right. And I think we'll manage to catch on soon enough."

Josh tossed jackets and hats and scarves to Drew, who began passing them down the line until they reached their owners.

Michael shrugged into his jacket, then helped Amber with hers.

"Thanks." She pulled on her hat and mittens and led him

through the front door. On the sidewalk in front of the house, they stood in the cold night air, waiting for everyone to join them. Or to be exact, everyone but Mom and Penny.

"Are you ready for this?" she asked Michael.

"I'm ready for anything."

She glanced sideways at him. He had tugged his ski cap down, framing his eyes, sending her gaze directly to his. The street lights reflecting off the snow made his eyes shimmer, adding a glow that brightened his entire face. A face she knew so well, and not just from the times he had stayed at the lodge.

On more nights than she could count, Michael played a starring role in her dreams. That secret pleasure made her eager to drift off to sleep at night. Even better, on those mornings after, she woke with a smile on her lips…until she opened her eyes and reality hit.

Blinking, she looked away. Her family paired up to head toward the house where the carolers would meet. Michael reached for her mittened hand.

"What are you doing?" she asked.

"What do you think? Saving you from getting drafted into that meet-market competition."

"Well, thanks for riding to my rescue, Prince Charming. But at the moment, nobody's watching. We're practically alone. Look, everyone's getting ahead of us."

"And when they discover we're missing and look back to find us, what do you want them to see?"

She flushed at the pictures flashing through her mind. A couple sharing a laugh…a hug…a kiss… What more could a girl ask to make her star-studded Christmas evening complete?

Of course, the visions were just more dreams. When that girl stood wide-awake, eyes open, out in the bracing air, she found the strength to keep from getting caught up in fantasies. *Or else.* "I don't want my family to see anything."

Before she could pull free, he tucked her hand in the crook of his arm and started walking.

Fantasy warred with reality in a one-sided battle. But nothing could win out over the truth. A week from now, Michael would be gone from her life again. Abruptly, she said, "Do you want me to take down the tree at the lodge tomorrow?"

"The day after Christmas?" He sounded surprised. "What's the hurry? Is this when you'd take down your tree at home?"

"No. We always leave it up past New Year's. Through Little Christmas, January sixth, as a matter of fact."

Last year, he had hit her with a double whammy. Along with turning down her request to play Santa, he'd cancelled his plans to come to Snowflake Valley the week of the party. Needing something to cheer her up, she had left the tree standing in the lodge almost the entire month of January. Even worse, this year, he had accepted her request, then backed out. Who knew when she would finally be ready to put away the decorations?

But she didn't own the lodge.

"Since you'll be around," she said, "I thought you might rather have the tree gone."

He shrugged. "Whatever you want to do with it is fine. But wouldn't you like a break from all the Christmas cheer?" He gestured at the strands of red and green lights twined around the lampposts. "It's everywhere you look in this town. Don't folks who live here like to get it out of their houses, at least?"

"Not me. I love it. And now I have a question for *you*. I heard you talking with my dad as we were leaving. You were awfully quick to say you'll attend the opening ceremony of the festival with us tomorrow. What happened to having so much work with you?" Again, that grim, tight-lipped expression crossed his face. She didn't like seeing the change. Or, worse, knowing she'd caused it. "Besides," she rushed on, "I'd think you would run as far as you could from anything to do with the festival."

"Because I'm a Scrooge?" He gave her a crooked smile. "Yeah, normally I'd take a pass. I'm only going along with that for you, too."

Prince Charming, all right. From her hand on his arm to the tips of her toes, warmth spread through her. Afraid he would see her reaction in her face, she looked away. She couldn't believe in a fairytale that, for her, wouldn't come with a happy ending.

Keep it light. Keep it real. As they passed another lamppost, she gestured toward it. "Speaking of decorations everywhere we look, I suppose I should warn you. Before the ceremony, we're all going out for lunch to celebrate Lyssa and Nick's engagement."

"No problem. I like to eat."

"At the Candy Cane?"

He groaned.

"I'm *so* sorry."

"Yeah. I can tell by the size of your grin. I'll bet you love that place."

"Down to the last tiny ornament."

"The Candy Cane." He shook his head. "Whoever came up with a name like that for a diner?"

"Anatole, the owner. And for your information, the Snowflake Valley Chamber of Commerce approved it unanimously. The name is good for business, plus it goes along with the Christmas cheer. Which, by the way, *we* call 'adding a little touch of magic.'"

"I call it being a little touched in the head."

"*Michael.*"

He laughed and squeezed her hand.

Being so close to him, laughing with him, teasing him… she'd done all those things so many times before. In her dreams.

Keep it real. Could things get any more real than *this*?

Keep this *for as long as you can.*

"Come on, everyone's waiting for us." She pulled her hand from his arm and grinned up at him. "Last one to Santa's mailbox has to make hot chocolate tonight."

• • •

While Michael put the SUV away in the garage, Amber settled Penny in the playpen. Though it was nearly ten o'clock after a long day, the baby was still wide-eyed and excited.

Like mother, like daughter.

Smiling, Amber went to turn on the tree lights. The perfect touch for the best Christmas ever. The twinkling lights in the room matched the lights inside her. Who wouldn't have felt a little glow with a man like Michael by her side? So what if she had only a week before her prince left town? By then, anything could happen.

At the sound of the kitchen door closing, she wrapped her arms around herself. The hug did nothing to settle her excitement. Her heart raced, but for a much different reason than when Michael had arrived…only last night?

As he entered the living room, he took one look at her and frowned. "Are you cold? Want me to start a fire?"

You already have. But who would say no to an invitation like that one? Curled up together on the couch in front of the fireplace, who knew how hot things would get. "That would be great. I haven't thawed out from our walk through town."

"You should have said something on the ride home. I'd have cranked up the heat in the SUV." He knelt in front of the fireplace. "Another thing you forgot to mention—that

Christmas caroling gig. Were you afraid I'd turn down your invitation to it in front of your entire family?"

"Try complete panic. What if you'd insisted on auditioning for them—and not been able to carry a tune?"

"Surprised you, huh?"

"That's an understatement. You didn't mention one single word about a tryout."

He turned to scowl at her over his shoulder. "Very funny."

She smiled. After a pause, she said, "Did you have a good time today?"

"Yeah, I did."

Now who was surprised? The trace of emotion in his tone made her hopes soar. Forget memories and dreams. Focus on miracles. If Michael could learn to enjoy the holidays and get comfortable being around her family, what else might he come to like? "Don't sound so shocked," she told him. "We're not *that* bad." She laughed softly, not wanting to disturb Penny.

Michael crossed the room to her, and the laugh caught in her throat.

"Some of you aren't bad at all," he said.

"I'll take that as a compliment."

"You should." He reached for her hand. She hadn't realized nerves had left her toying with the zipper tab of her knitted jacket. Warmth from his fingers heated hers. "Want some help taking off your sweater?" She'd heard that same teasing tone this morning when she'd wondered if he meant to flirt with her.

No wondering now. And her imagination wasn't working overtime. The curve of his lips and the gleam in his eyes told her he was going for the full flirt. And more. Slowly, he unzipped her jacket. With every inch the tab lowered, the higher her excitement climbed.

Words like *boss* and *employee*, *paycheck*, and

independence, filled her mind. She brushed them away like snowflakes, leaving room for words like *anticipation* and *possibilities* and *together*.

Michael tugged at the final inch of the zipper. A shiver ran down her spine.

Once he'd helped her slip out of the jacket, he tossed it onto the couch. He moved a half step toward her, close enough for her to feel the heat from his body. His lips curved another few degrees.

"Beautiful," he murmured. His gaze held hers for a long, silent moment, then drifted to her mouth. She could read his thoughts. They echoed hers.

The sparks inside her burst into fireworks, consuming every caution she could give herself, every warning she wanted to obey. For months, she had imagined what it would be like to have Michael kiss her.

She held her breath, watching…wanting…even willing to make the next move.

The warmth of his lips on hers, oh so briefly, sent a rush of pure pleasure through her. With one finger, he traced a strand of hair brushing her cheek. "As late as it is, I wasn't sure you'd want to come all the way back up here to stay the night."

"Of course," she said softly. "I told you, I don't have anywhere else to go. Or anywhere else I'd rather be." She wanted to wrap her arms around Michael, to have him wrap his arms around her and hold her forever. But for now, she'd take another kiss. Smiling in anticipation, she stared up at him.

He lowered his hand and stepped back.

"I'm sorry," he said. "I shouldn't have teased you or touched you. And I sure as heck shouldn't have kissed you. As you said tonight, there's nobody here to see us now. This isn't real."

"It feels real to me." She gestured around them. "Lights flashing on the tree. The fire crackling. I can even smell the pine garlands on the mantel." All things she loved about the holiday.

And in front of her stood the man she loved more than Christmas.

No teasing. No doubts. No going back. In her heart she knew she had loved him all along.

"I meant us," he said. "Being together. We both know that's not real." He took another step back. "I think I'll call it a night."

Nodding, she watched until he disappeared from sight up the stairs. She glanced from the crackling fire to the cozy couch. The empty couch.

Not exactly the way she'd expected the night to end. But what was one night, when she still had hopes of forever.

• • •

The next morning, Amber drove down into the valley to leave Penny with her parents. After running a few errands in town, she went alone to the Candy Cane. Well, not completely alone. Thoughts of Michael shared the ride with her.

At the lodge, she had come downstairs determined to act like herself around him. Her normal housekeeper-not-woman-in-love-with-you self. Hard enough to do when she felt sure he'd see the love shining from her eyes. Impossible to accomplish when she couldn't find him.

Finally, she spotted the note on the kitchen table.

He had already eaten breakfast and gone off to the ski slopes.

So much for having work to do. So much for promising her dad he would join them for the opening ceremony for the festival. How she would explain his absence to her family, she didn't know.

As she had told Michael, Christmas and New Year's weeks were the busiest of all in Snowflake Valley. The Candy Cane's parking lot proved that point. With the lot nearly filled to capacity, she wedged her small car into a sliver of space.

When she opened the diner's front door, a wave combined of warm air, mouthwatering scents, and ringing voices washed over her. From behind the front counter, Anatole, the diner's owner and chief cook, sent her a smile and a nod. She veered in that direction.

"How are you, gorgeous?" he asked.

"Hungry," she shot back.

"Good." Anatole slapped his ample waistline, covered by his apron. Almost as round as he was tall, the man was perpetually jolly. The locals teased that once his jet-black hair and mustache turned white, he would be elected Snowflake Valley's chief Santa. "You'll find plenty to your liking on the menu today."

"I always do," she assured him.

"Your gang's already seated in the back room."

"Thanks." Smiling, she made her way through the diner, pausing to say a quick hello to many of the locals.

Garlands and ornaments and twinkling lights decorated the entire room. While some of them were additions brought out for the holiday season, most stayed up for visitors year-round. She loved the Candy Cane and every Christmas-themed business in town, even when the stores were filled with people she didn't know. Maybe especially then, because she appreciated the idea of complete strangers enjoying her hometown.

Why couldn't Michael be like them?

How long would it take to win him over?

In the doorway of the rear dining room, she came to a screeching halt. Her heart matched that with its own little skid-step. Her family had claimed the largest table. All seats but one had been taken. The one beside Michael.

After reading the note he'd left that morning, she had never expected him to show up here.

He was half-turned away from her, talking to her dad, and she took an extra few seconds to look him over. Taller and broader-shouldered than anyone at the table, he was hard to miss. His light-green sweater made his hair and eyes look black as coal.

He glanced in her direction, and his gaze met hers. Her throat tightened, her breath caught, and her stomach did a little flip as though she were six years old again and turning somersaults in the backyard. As he continued to hold her gaze, she struggled to remind herself he sat surrounded by her family, some of whom had to be looking her way now, too.

Sure enough, Lyssa waved, flailing her arm in Amber's sightline, breaking the spell.

Not sure whether to be happy or sorry for her sister's interference, she hurried across the room. She took her seat between Penny and Michael. With a party of twelve including Penny, space was even tighter here than it had been at Christmas dinner. As Michael shifted in his chair, he bumped against her.

"Excuse me," he said. "I guess this table wasn't made for people with elbows."

She laughed…until he reached over to drape his arm across the back of her chair. Well, of course. They had an audience again.

She could feel the warmth of his hand just inches from her shoulder. The scent of his aftershave, something with a hint of spice, made her long to close her eyes and take a deep breath. With suddenly trembling fingers, she grabbed a menu from the table in front of her. Not that she needed to look at the dinner options. She could have recited each of Anatole's

Christmasy-titled items from memory.

As if she had broken another spell, everyone reached for their menus and began discussing what they planned to eat.

Her hands still shaky, Amber leaned over to say hello to Penny. Her shoulder grazed Michael's fingertips. Yet again, a pleasurable shiver ran through her, followed by a realization that hadn't hit her till now.

Yesterday was a holiday dinner. Today was a *date.*

Granted, it was a group date. And except for Penny, she would rather have had the group stay home. She loved her family. She just didn't need them along on her first—and most likely only—date with Michael.

What a horrible thought. Flushing, she stared down at the table. They were here to celebrate Lyssa and Nick's engagement, not to bring *her* fantasies to life.

"You okay?" Michael asked in a low voice.

She started. "Yes, I'm fine. Why?"

"You turned red all of a sudden."

"Oh." She fanned herself with the menu. "It's a little warm in here."

"You think so?" He had lowered his voice, adding a huskiness to it that turned her tiny white lie into nothing but the truth. "Want some help taking off your jacket?"

Her gaze shot to his. He'd asked her the same thing last night, but now he'd raised the flirt factor. His dark eyes were gleaming, and his mouth curved in a sexy, one-sided smile. Her cheeks grew hotter yet. Her palms felt suddenly damp. She brushed them across her lap.

"No, I'm fine, thank you." Except for her wild imagination. "And wow," she murmured, so low he had to bend closer to hear, "you're good at this pretend stuff."

"That's not all I'm good at," he whispered into her ear.

A little warm didn't come close to describing the heat wave now rushing through her.

Chapter Seven

While they finished their lunch, Michael looked around the diner. Anything to keep from giving in and getting closer to Amber. She had always drawn him in, but leaning down to hear her soft voice had almost sent him toppling into her lap.

He studied the room. If not for his promise to help Amber, to pretend to be her date, he could easily have written off this lunch.

She might have hit it right when she had called him Scrooge. As far as he was concerned, all the holiday decorations on the walls had to go. The Santa and Mrs. Claus salt and pepper shakers sitting on the tables could follow. The ornaments dangling from the light fixtures above their heads only added to his reasons for disliking this place.

And the kicker—the dishes listed on the menu.

Reindeer Roast Beef and Snowball Smashed Potatoes. Yuletide Yams. Santa's Favorite Fries.

And he'd thought the *Candy Cane* was a bad choice of name!

"What did you think of the Mistletoe Meatloaf?"

Amber's dad asked him.

With his fork, Michael flicked aside the large sprig of parsley that had been decorating his dinner, probably meant to represent the mistletoe. "Best I've ever eaten," he said truthfully. If only he could forget what it was called.

Evidently, he'd given the wrong answer. Mr. Barnett waved his hand and said, "You haven't tasted a good meatloaf until you've tried my wife's."

"Yeah," Drew said. "Mom makes the best ever."

High praise, coming from a teenager. Then again, teen boys loved their food. So did he. "Maybe your mom should pass her recipe along to the cook here at the…diner."

"Are you kidding?" Lyssa asked. Seated beside him, she looked up, her expression serious. "That meatloaf is a family secret."

On his other side, Amber shifted in her chair. No need to see her expression to read that reaction. She didn't like the reminder of her own secrets—her unpaid bill, the new living arrangements, their agreement about pretending to be a couple. All those had her on edge. He couldn't help wanting to calm her nerves.

Instead, he found the waitress holding a menu out to him. He ran his eye down the dessert list and made his choice. *Pumpkin Pie with Merry Little Marshmallows.* Just the thing.

He rested his arm on the back of Amber's chair again. His hand brushed her hair, and just that brief touch left his fingertips tingling. He wanted more.

Last night, tough as it had been, he'd done the right thing and backed away from her. But they were here today to put on a performance, weren't they? Gently, he tugged on one of her silky strands. "Sounds like you've been keeping things from me, Amber. Has your mom passed her meatloaf recipe down to you?"

She laughed, her eyes sparkling. Talk about being good

at playing a role. This woman was Oscar material. "Well," she said, "I *am* part of the family."

"I take it that's a yes. Good. You'll have to make it for me sometime."

Her smile froze, but only for a second. "I can do that."

"Oh, but look at this," Lyssa said suddenly. Now she was grinning at him. "Here's one thing Mom doesn't add to her meatloaf. Mistletoe." She took the sprig of parsley from his plate and dangled it over his head.

"Uh-oh," said one of the twins.

"You know what that means," said the other twin.

"I have to kiss Lyssa?" he asked.

"Hey, man," Nick said, "kiss your own woman."

Everyone at the table laughed. Except Amber, who stared at him, wide-eyed.

His own woman. Since he'd met her, he'd fought *not* to think of her that way. At first, she was married. Then, she was pregnant. Last and always, she was a mom focused on family.

He looked overhead. Lyssa waved the parsley. It wasn't real mistletoe, and he and Amber weren't really a couple. But her entire family sat watching. He'd started this whole "together" thing and now he had to see it through. With a quick kiss, that's all. For her sake.

He slid his arm around her shoulders. "Guess we've got to uphold a Christmas tradition, don't we?"

"Uh…"

No big deal. One quick kiss to satisfy her family. One kiss just long enough to feel the softness of her lips, to taste a trace of iced tea, to catch the scent of perfume so light he hadn't known she was wearing any, to hear… *Bells?*

No, not bells. The ringing of silverware against glass.

He sat back. Amber looked starry-eyed. The ringing died down, replaced by laughter.

"Thought you were never coming up for air," Nick said.

"Maybe Mom does need to add some mistletoe to her recipe," Lyssa said with a laugh.

"In any case," Mr. Barnett said, "Mom needs to put meatloaf on the menu one of these days. It's been a while since we've had it at home."

"It has," Mrs. Barnett agreed. "That's a good idea. I'll plan it for later this week. And Michael, you're invited for supper that night."

Earth to Michael. He blinked, refusing to look at Amber. "Thanks." He forced a smile. No sense announcing that no matter what night it was, they wouldn't need to set a chair at the table for him.

He'd gotten Amber off the hook with her family. But when it came to his feelings for her, he was still dangling like that phony mistletoe. Still fighting. Still trying to pretend those feelings didn't exist.

Time for a change of subject. "So, what does Snowflake Valley do for the grand opening—a ribbon-cutting ceremony?"

"Nothing that formal," Callie told him. "The mayor says a few words, this year I'll announce the auction, then Santa will arrive in his sleigh."

He managed not to roll his eyes. "Let me guess. It's pulled by eight tiny reindeer."

"Actually, it's motor-driven." Amber sounded steadier than he felt. "We were forced to do away with the reindeer idea. The horses standing in for them refused to wear their antlers."

"That's a real break with tradition."

"Sometimes you have to step outside the box."

"True. I've said that more than once in a staff meeting." He looked down at her, unable to give up another glimpse of her curved lips. How much more of a fool could he be? Though her smiles might have been genuine, they weren't meant for him.

For his own peace of mind—and his self-preservation—their acting gig had to end. He would break the news to her tonight. They wouldn't renege on any plans with Nick and Lyssa. But for the rest of the Barnetts, he and Amber would fall back on his excuse of all the work he'd brought along with him.

Yeah. That paperwork. A much better alternative than spending more time with Amber and her baby and her family.

The waitress set his dessert plate in front of him. He grabbed his fork and stabbed one of his *Merry Little Marshmallows*.

"Thank you for treating my family to lunch," Amber said. "You didn't have to do that."

Michael looked down at her. They were walking along the sidewalk outside the Candy Cane, headed for the community center. She had been all smiles ever since he'd kissed her.

As with the caroling last night, they'd fallen behind the rest of her family. Good. It gave them a chance to talk. "I was happy to pick up the lunch tab. I had already invited Nick and Lyssa out for a meal."

"But not everyone else."

"No problem. You all seem to come as a package deal."

"We do. Most of the time, anyway. And you have to admit it's a good deal, isn't it?"

Not for him. Not when it was a *family* package.

He couldn't have the conversation he wanted with her right here. Swallowing a sigh, he glanced down the street ahead of them. "How far is it we're going?"

"We've arrived." She gestured to a single-story, square building surrounded by a snow-covered lawn. "This is the community center."

They followed the rest of her family into the building.

A short, broad-shouldered man he recognized from previous visits to Snowflake Valley immediately headed their way. Mayor Corrigan held out his hand. "Michael. I'd heard you were in town and had planned to look you up. How long are you here?"

"Till January second." One week from today.

"Excellent." The mayor beamed. He glanced at his watch. "We're not due to start the festivities for a few minutes. If you can spare me a moment, I have a proposition I'd like to discuss with you."

"Fine." Though odd. He'd never done business with anyone in Snowflake Valley. What would the mayor want with him? A glance around him showed the entire Barnett family—plus Nick—must have wondered the same thing.

Mayor Corrigan gestured to the opposite side of the room. "Come this way. We can chat in the office."

"I'll see you later—" Amber began.

"Not at all," the mayor said. "I wanted to speak with you, too, Amber."

Michael exchanged a quick glance with her. She seemed as puzzled as he was.

In the room at the end of the hallway, the mayor ushered them to seats and took a chair behind a large desk. He rested his palms flat on the desktop. "I'll come directly to the point. Michael, the town council is looking to hire a firm to update the decorations here in town. We'd like you to consider the job."

"Thanks." Again, he stopped short of rolling his eyes. "But I'm not a decorator. I'm in electronics."

"Precisely. It's the electronic displays I'm talking about."

Plenty of those in this town. The job could turn into a lucrative contract, especially for a small, privately-owned company. "You're talking about the displays all through Snowflake Valley," he clarified.

"Every one of them. We do regular upkeep and maintenance, of course. But it's been quite some time since they've had an overhaul."

"That doesn't sound like just a job pushing papers," Amber said quietly.

A stronger man might not have caved, but one look at those eyes, now shining again, did him in. Touching her temple with one fingertip, he brushed away a lock of hair.

The mayor cleared his throat. Startled, Michael turned back to him.

"We're talking about more than mere cosmetic changes. We'd like to upgrade some of the displays to laser light systems."

Michael nodded. The town's plans would involve much more than just new installation. He sat forward. "You're looking for someone who will bring in their own designs?"

"Exactly—while staying true to the old-fashioned ambience of Snowflake Valley, of course," the mayor finished hastily.

"Of course." He tried to keep his tone level. "I'm sure I could come up with a proposal that would satisfy your council members."

"I'm sure you could, too. We've done our research, and you come highly recommended."

"Thanks for the vote of confidence."

Mayor Corrigan raised a hand in caution. "Naturally, we'd have to open the job for bidding. But we want more than a low-ball price." He smiled. "We want the right man for the job, and I'm certain that's you."

Beside him, he could see Amber gripping her hands together in her lap. She couldn't be feeling the same rising excitement he was…could she?

"It's good that you're here right now," the mayor said. "You'll need to see the town from top to bottom in order to submit a comprehensive bid. More important, the council members want to see you're interested in Snowflake Valley. The best way to show them that is to get involved in everything going on during the town's busiest season." He smiled broadly. "I can't think of any better way to show you're the right candidate and to prove your interest than by taking part in the biggest annual event we hold just for our citizens."

Hearing Amber's indrawn breath, Michael stiffened. She knew what was coming. Nothing good.

"'Course, I'm a bit biased." The mayor's *aw-shucks* delivery confirmed Michael's suspicion. "The Snow Ball gets a lot of press, and as you know, good press is good news for any small town."

"I'm happy to make a donation."

The man waved the suggestion away. "No, sir. While your contribution will be greatly appreciated, it's not your money that'll prove your worth to the council. It's your willingness to participate." He smiled again. "I want you to run for Snow Ball King."

Now he knew how Amber had felt when Callie wanted to put her in the royal hot seat. "I can't do that."

"'Course, you can. There's nothing to it. Just show up at the major functions in town, shake a few hands, pat a few babies' heads."

"I'm only here for a week."

"And the voting's held on New Year's Eve. You'll be here."

Or else. He also knew a veiled threat when he heard one. Either run for the position or get run out of town, so to speak, as far as being awarded that contract.

The trouble was, he had to admit the mayor's proposition had already snagged his interest. The job intrigued him more than anything had in years. The scope of it. The fun of working with the latest technology. The challenge of designing and creating new displays himself…not that he was wild about Santa sleighs and reindeer.

A knock sounded on the office door. "Come in," the mayor called.

A tense-looking woman stood in the doorway. "Mayor, we're in a stalemate up front, and your vote's the tiebreaker. It will only take a minute."

"I'll be right there." The woman disappeared from sight, and Mayor Corrigan turned back to him. "I take it we have an understanding. Mind you, you don't have to win the competition, Michael, just participate. And naturally, with you running for Snow King, I'll nominate Amber as Queen."

She gasped. "Mayor, I can't accept that."

"'Course, you can," he said again.

"But I…Michael and I aren't eligible. We're…together."

"So I've heard."

Word sure got around in this town.

The mayor leaned forward, staring deliberately at Amber's clasped hands. "I don't see any engagement ring on your finger. And if you're not officially spoken for, my dear, you're eligible for my nomination."

Lyssa must not have known about this little loophole.

Amber stared at him.

He froze. She couldn't expect him now to go out and buy her a ring…could she?

"Sit tight," the mayor said. "I'll be back in a few minutes."

• • •

Once the door swung closed behind Mayor Corrigan, Amber "sat tight" for as long as she could. Three seconds, max. Then she whipped around to face Michael. "You *have* to do this."

His hands went up in protest. "Whoa. Hold on, Amber. Playing at being a couple's one thing. Acting like some fairytale characters, just to get your family off your back—"

"That's not the point."

"It isn't?"

"No."

"You don't actually want us to become King and Queen?"

"Of course not." *Of course, yes.* What little girl growing up in Snowflake Valley—growing up *anywhere*—wouldn't want to be Queen of the Snow Ball? And with the possibility of being Queen to Michael's King? How could she turn down that chance?

Which made it a huge struggle to tell yet another little white lie. But this time, she would willingly sacrifice one of her childhood dreams for something now much more important. She would even stop thinking about their kiss at the Candy Cane…for the moment. "You want that contract, Michael."

He laughed. "You would say that. You believe Snowflake Valley's the greatest thing since—"

"No. That's not what I meant, either. This is all about *you*. You *want* that job. That's all there is to it."

He frowned, as if he suspected she'd had a hand in the mayor's offer. "Why? What do you know about it?"

"Nothing about the town's plans. But I know how you reacted when Mayor Corrigan laid everything out to you. Don't tell me the idea didn't catch your interest. You gave yourself away. Your voice…your body language… You looked as if you were ready to get down to work right that minute."

"I'll admit, there were some things about the project that intrigued me."

"Right. Like, no paperwork."

"There will always be paperwork," he said dryly.

She laughed. "You know what I mean. Instead of being just a paper-pusher, the way you'd said you are, you'll be able to get hands-on with this project." And maybe need to spend more time in Snowflake Valley.

"Getting awarded that contract could make a big difference. It'll relieve some of the boredom, anyhow. But I'm sure you got the mayor's point. I'll be in the running for the project only as long as I run in the competition."

"He also said it's not that hard."

"I'll bet."

"You won't be alone. I'll be right there beside you."

"Will you?" One eyebrow went up. "You have to know what this will mean. We'll be playing to a packed house. To the whole town, not just to your family."

"I can do that."

"You think so? Shake a few hands and all the rest of it… Right. You also heard the mayor say word's gotten around about us being together. You think the gossips spreading that word won't be watching us?"

"I can handle that."

"Yeah? What happens when we're out in public?"

"We…we'll act just the way we've been acting."

"You mean, like at the Candy Cane? Because I have a feeling the residents of Snowflake Valley want to see some sparks between a prospective King and Queen."

She took a deep breath to steady her voice. Forget his running for Snow Ball King. Let him see how she really felt, and most likely he would run all the way home to California. "I can do sparks." With her eyes closed. Just the way she had when Michael had kissed her.

"You mean pretend to do sparks."

"Yes. Pretend." Those little white lies grew bigger all the time.

"All right." He nodded. "After all, it's only for a week. So why don't we both just relax and have a good time."

The door behind them swung open.

Mayor Corrigan entered the room and took his seat again. He smiled at them both. “Well, you two. What’ll it be? Are we adding your names to the Snow Ball ballot?”

“Yes,” Amber said firmly, all her hopes and dreams wrapped up in that one little word. She didn’t want to have a good time with Michael. Well…yes, she did. But she wanted much more than that. In the one short week ahead, she wanted him to come to love Snowflake Valley…and her family…and her baby…and her…just as much as she loved him.

Forget winning the Snow Ball Queen crown. She wanted to win *Michael.*

Michael, who hadn’t said a word. He sat watching her again, as if he could read every thought going through her mind. And still, he didn’t answer.

Her heart thudded. Maybe she would lose the race before it even started. Maybe she’d asked for too many miracles at once. Maybe her Prince Charming would turn out to be—

Don’t even think it.

Michael turned to the mayor. “Count me in.”

Chapter Eight

When Amber arrived back at the lodge with Penny after the brief opening ceremony, Michael's SUV was already in the garage. Fresh snow had fallen during the afternoon, making the walk to the house even more of a challenge.

Downstairs, Michael was nowhere to be found. Not a bad thing. A little outdoor exercise would help burn up some of her excess energy. Leaving Penny asleep in her playpen in the living room, she grabbed the baby monitor and went outside to shovel the path.

After setting the monitor on the porch railing, she took a deep breath of frigid air. Maybe that would clear the whirlwind of thoughts in her head. And there were lots of thoughts swirling around in there, of Michael's kiss beneath the mistletoe and the competition and the possible contract.

Just as she dug her shovel into the lightly packed snow, she heard boots thumping on the wooden porch, followed by the thud of the back door.

"Need some help?" Michael called.

"No, thanks. The snow's not that heavy." *Don't scare the*

man off. Deliberately, she loaded the shovel and dropped the mound of snow a few feet from the walkway.

A *chh-chhhh-chh* sound made her look up. He had taken the long-handled broom she had left propped against the railing and was brushing snow from the back steps.

"You don't need to do that," she protested. "That's my job."

"It's my lodge," he countered, smiling, "and I'm your boss."

As if she needed the reminder. Or maybe she did, judging by the way her pulse had immediately jumped in response to that smile. Shrugging, she went back to work. The *chh-chhhh-chh* sound continued for a few minutes, but soon dead silence followed.

Seconds later, the *thwack* of a lightly packed snowball exploded against her shoulder. She whirled to find Michael grinning. "What was that for?"

"Rule number one. Never turn your back on an opponent when there's snow around."

As if she hadn't already known that. "Well, here's rule number two. Never throw a snowball at someone with better aim." While she'd spoken, she had knelt to scoop up a handful of snow, watching Michael as he did the same. She timed her missile to hit just as he stood upright. The snowball burst against his chest. "Score!"

As he raised his arm, she ducked. His snowball sailed two feet over her head.

"Rookie!" she called, laughing. "I had a better arm when I was in kindergarten."

"Oh, yeah? Ever have your face washed with snow?"

"Not by you. And I never will." When she crouched for another handful of snow, Michael advanced, his long legs suddenly closing half the space between them. Squealing, she turned to run—and tripped over the handle of the shovel.

As she went down, Michael tackled her, sliding one arm around her waist. Before she could hit the drifts of snow, he rolled, pulling her against him, cushioning her fall. She landed lightly on the ground beside him.

"Unfair," she declared, gasping to catch her breath. "This isn't football."

"All's fair in a snowball fight," he countered. He scooped up a mound of snow in one gloved hand. "About that face-washing."

"You wouldn't dare."

"Wouldn't I?"

"Oh, pretty please, Michael…" She clasped her hands together in a pleading gesture. As he returned her smile, she knocked his arm away. His handful of snow sprayed across the ground. She laughed. "And about the power of distraction…"

"You fight dirty."

"No, I fight to win."

"So do I." He took her hand. Then he lowered his head toward hers. He stopped with his mouth just inches from her lips. She shivered, but not from the snow beneath them. "*Now* tell me what I wouldn't dare."

Did she have the nerve to say it?

Did she have the strength not to?

"You wouldn't dare kiss me," she blurted.

"Wouldn't I?"

Oh, pretty please, Michael…

He brushed her mouth with his. Once. Twice. Three times. More than enough to tantalize. Not enough to satisfy.

She was ready to dare him to do more when he stood, pulling her to her feet along with him. "It's too cold to have you lying out here in the snow."

Visions of the living room couch in front of the fire… her cozy bed upstairs…his king-size mattress in the master suite…all danced like sugarplums before her eyes. Wishful thinking. But oh, what good wishes.

"We should go inside," he said.

"Quitting already? My boss wouldn't be too happy to see that."

He gestured toward the lodge. "*My* boss would have noticed the job was done."

Sure enough, the back steps and porch were cleared of snow. She tilted her head, eyeing him as they walked the few feet to the house.

"What? Whatever that look means, I don't like it."

"It means who knew you were such a good worker." Leaning against the porch railing, she smiled up at him and added encouragingly, "We could really use another good worker to help with the festival."

"Shouldn't all these celebrations be done by now? Christmas is over."

"It's *never* over in Snowflake Valley. We have visitors all year round. And the festival is the biggest draw of the year. Plus, Callie has the silent auction planned. So we need even more help than usual."

"Not from me. Getting close to all that cheer wouldn't be good for me."

"Of course it would. Where's your heart?" she demanded.

"In my wallet. Right where you'll find the donation I'll be happy to make."

"That would be great. But we could also use a strong back and an extra pair of hands." If there was a wheedling tone to her voice, who could blame her? She had to help her family, and she wanted him by her side. Time was short.

That alone made it worth a little negotiation.

She propped her boot on the bottom step. He took a seat that left them eye-to-eye. Almost mouth-to-mouth again. Despite the cold air, she felt a flash of warmth. She loosened the scarf she wore draped around her neck.

"After we're done working," she said encouragingly, "there's time off for good behavior."

"And I know just what to do with it." He tugged on the scarf. "You're too tempting," he murmured. "I want to kiss you, even when there's no mistletoe around."

His gaze went to her mouth. Her knees went weak. *Either kiss me or catch me when I fall.*

He looked up at her, his eyes mesmerizing. But his smile suddenly looked as unsteady as she felt. "What happens if I'm not on my best behavior at all times?"

Who cared about that now? Right this minute, all she wanted was to lean forward. To give him what *he* wanted. A kiss.

As if he had changed his mind, Michael leaned back to rest his elbows on the step behind him, breaking eye contact. Breaking the spell.

Swallowing her disappointment, she forced a grin. "Don't worry, there will be enough of my family around to make sure you stay focused on the job." Too true. Unfortunately. "But it won't be all work and no play. And don't forget the Snow Ball on New Year's Eve. Drinks—well, soft drinks—the party's at the community center, after all. Anyway, drinks and dinner, dancing, maybe something fabulous from the auction." And of course, the chance to become Michael's Queen. "Life just doesn't get any better."

"Are you sure about that?"

She tried—and failed—to push away the memories of what he had said that afternoon.

So why don't we both just relax and have a good time.

It's only for a week.

No matter how much she loved this man, she had to worry about next week and the next and all the weeks after that. About her *real* life, with her daughter. Her job. Her future. The one she couldn't risk by making yet another mistake with another man. Especially this man, who issued her paycheck.

She wanted Michael. But he wasn't part of her real life. Of her world. How could she ever have believed only one week would change that?

She resettled her scarf. "Well," she said finally, "I know it's not the high life you're used to back in California, but for this small-town girl, the festival and the Snow Ball are both pretty exciting events."

She glanced past him up the steps to the front door. So close, yet so far. "I need to go check on Penny."

"She hasn't let out a squawk. I've been monitoring the monitor." He laughed. "But to tell you the truth, I feel confident we'd hear her without it."

"Very funny—not."

His dark gaze met hers again. Her determination to stay away from him melted like snowflakes hitting a hot stove.

Not good at all. What kind of role model was she going to be for her daughter?

Taking a deep breath, she brushed past him and went up the steps to the back door.

Considering Michael had stayed closed up in his office the rest of the afternoon, Amber wasn't sure he would be interested in supper. Seeing him walk into the kitchen came as a surprise.

Then again, everyone had to eat.

On her way home that afternoon, she had picked up more leftovers at her parents' house. The containers sat lined up on the kitchen counter. "Just give me a few minutes to organize," she said. That was it. Be businesslike. Professional. The perfect cook and housekeeper. "I'll get the table in the dining area ready while everything's reheating."

"Don't worry about it. Let's eat in here. That'll be less trouble for us both."

"But the dining area's decorated for the holiday."

"And the holiday's over."

He didn't sound at all upset by that. She thought wistfully of the Christmas party she had held here for the kids and of the decorations she had put up in the combined dining and living area. A poinsettia and candles. Garland. Crystal snowflakes. And in the corner of the living room, the Christmas tree, sparkling with light.

Frowning, she glanced around the kitchen. "In here, about the only thing hinting at the holiday is the green dishtowel."

"What difference does that make? We're not eating the towels."

She had to laugh.

"Besides," he went on, "it makes more sense to stay here, instead of setting up that big table just for the two of us." He glanced over at the playpen. "Make that the three of us."

She shrugged, giving in gracefully. After she put the leftovers in the oven, she crossed to the doorway. "Be right back. I just want to grab a few table decorations to liven things up."

He shook his head but simply reached across to grab the notebook she had left on the counter. The book listed all the jobs she did on a regular basis, as well as any problems that popped up. It didn't seem possible she had worked for Michael for more than a year. But one look at her daughter provided the proof.

She gathered what she wanted from the dining area. Back in the kitchen, she draped a runner across the oak table, then added a small poinsettia in a pot shaped like Santa's sleigh.

Michael glanced up from her notebook. "Is this sleigh motor-driven, like the one at the community center?"

"No. This one's powered by elves."

He laughed and returned his attention to the book.

While they ate, they discussed notes she had made. He left the running and maintenance of the lodge in her hands. She was proud of his trust, as proud as she was of her ability to take care of herself and Penny.

Not that she'd done very well in that department lately.

When they had finished eating, Michael sat back and glanced over at the empty plastic containers on the counter. "Guess I've put a dent in your leftovers. I'll have to make it up to you, take you out for another meal."

A real date. The thought warmed her all over. But she refused to let him know how much his offer thrilled her. Refused to hang on to the feeling at all. "That's okay. A week from now, my mom will have another roast turkey, along with a ham."

"Your family makes a big deal of New Year's, too?"

"Of course." She stared at him for a moment. He'd already told her about his horrible Christmases. "Doesn't your family try to make any of the holidays special?"

"No," he said shortly, pushing her notebook aside.

No wonder he acted like such a Scrooge.

"I'm sorry to hear that," she said softly.

"Don't be sorry. That's just the way it is. I suppose your family makes a big deal of every holiday on the calendar."

"Just about. We've had huge celebrations ever since I can remember, for any holiday you can name. And don't even get me started on birthdays." She smiled wryly. "Include everyone in my family, and we have *something* to celebrate almost every time I stop in to visit."

"And now you have Penny's birthday in the mix, too."

"Yes."

After a moment, he said, "When I hired you, you didn't tell me you were pregnant."

"No. I'd just found out myself not too long before that. And I hadn't told anyone yet." Except her husband…who had left her. At the interview, she had decided not to say anything about the baby. She couldn't. Not when she hadn't even told her family.

Michael had come to the lodge with guests last spring. Too late for skiing. Also too late for him to miss her growing belly. If she had told him at the interview, would he still have hired her?

What did that matter now? She grabbed her plate and reached across the table for his. "Ready for dessert?"

"You don't need to wait on me. This isn't a house party."

"I know," she said uncomfortably. "It's not a party at all. I'm sorry I interfered with your plans for solitude."

"You did throw my entire schedule off-track, didn't you? I suppose I should throw *you* out." No smile now.

She took the dishes to the sink and began rinsing them. "Listen to you," she forced herself to say lightly. "As if I'd really believe you would toss a mom and her baby out in the snow." The image made her think of their snowball fight. And what had come after.

A wet dinner plate nearly slipped from her hands. *Focus, already.* Easy to say. Impossible to do. But let him see just how he affected her, and she was in big trouble.

"Before I left town this afternoon," he said, "Nick and I made plans."

"Plans?"

"Yeah. He and Lyssa are coming up tomorrow for some skiing. They'll be here early. She said she has the rest of the week off from work."

She nodded. "It's a busy week at Holidaze—the gift shop she manages. But she wanted to spend the time with Nick while she could."

"They're planning to be here for breakfast."

"*Breakfast?*" That got her full attention. Time to do her job. Or better said, to 'fess up that she *hadn't* done it. "I completely forgot about going to the store today. We don't have enough here to feed them."

"I told Nick that. He said they would take care of it." He rose from his seat. "I need to get some work done."

She frowned. He couldn't have suddenly developed a passion for paperwork, could he? No. Short answer, he was avoiding her.

She watched him leave the room.

Even with him gone from view, she could still envision his smile. The one that lit his entire face, making him hotter than ever.

The one she hadn't seen since he'd asked about her pregnancy...and her family...and the holidays.

Chapter Nine

Amber set out frying pans and spatulas and measuring cups. She prepared the coffeemaker and lined up mugs on the counter. Anything to keep from glancing across the room.

More often than not, she lost the battle.

She hadn't seen Michael again last night, but when she and Penny had come downstairs that morning, he was in the kitchen. Now, he stood gathering silverware from the drawer.

She frowned. When he brought guests to the lodge, he never helped her with any of the housework. It didn't seem right to have him in here. It didn't *feel* right, when she had spent half the night telling herself she needed to keep her distance.

"Really," she said, "I can manage. You don't have to do this. After all, you're the boss."

A good reminder to herself–and a good reason she shouldn't be wishing for his kiss.

He shrugged. "No problem. I want to work up a good appetite by the time Nick and Lyssa get here. I'm looking forward to *Elf Eggs Benedict*."

Again, she frowned. "I thought they'd just pick up some groceries at the store. Nick said they're bringing breakfast from the Candy Cane?"

"You're kidding me, right? I made that up. No, wait. You're not kidding." He rolled his eyes. "What do they call the bacon? *Santa's Sleigh Strips*?"

"*Jingle-Bell Bacon*. And don't make fun, Michael. Kids *love* reading the names of everything on the menu. So do their parents. If you weren't such a Scrooge—"

At the sound of car doors slamming, she killed that thought and pushed aside the curtain over the sink…then cringed. *Oh, no.* Michael would kill *her*.

A caravan had arrived.

After a glance through the window, he stared down at her, his expression unreadable. "Looks like your family decided to make breakfast a team sport."

"Looks like it," she agreed.

"Did you have a hand in this surprise?"

"*No.* I didn't even know you'd confirmed the plans with Nick until you told me." And then he had walked off to his office.

"Well, before they get in here…about what happened outside yesterday—"

"Forget about it," she blurted. "It was no big deal." Nothing close to what she longed for, anyway. And *nothing* was what she should expect from Michael.

He owned a company, a private ski lodge, and a townhouse in San Diego. She was a single mom who couldn't pay her electric bill. Worse from her perspective, he hated Christmas and didn't want anything to do with marriage or family.

"Nothing much happened," she said firmly, "and nothing else will. We'll keep pretending until…until we don't need to anymore." And stop the silly wishing for a happy ending.

She would swear he sagged in relief.

The door to the back porch swept open. Bright sunshine filled the kitchen. A clean cold breeze swept inside with enough force to ruffle the curtains. The change in temperature barely registered on her skin. Michael's blank features had already given her a chill.

The twins burst into the kitchen. As usual when they were excited, Mandy and Brooke talked over each other, one finishing the other's sentences.

"We all decided to come for breakfast—"

"—and we brought everything we need. Then after—"

"—we're going skiing. Except Callie and Lyssa—"

"—because they're going to start the posters for the auction. And except Mom—"

"—because she's going to watch Penny while they work."

By this time, the rest of her family and Nick had entered the kitchen. He unloaded a grocery sack onto the counter. "We've brought everything anyone could want for breakfast."

"Yes." Mom smiled up at Michael. "Good morning. You were so nice about treating for lunch yesterday, we all decided to come along with Lyssa and Nick and return the favor. Breakfast is on us."

"So is supper," Dad announced. "We're having Mom's meatloaf tonight and her sweet potato casserole."

She shot a glance at Michael, who stood smiling back at her mom as if he couldn't think of anything he'd like better. "But, Dad," she protested, "Michael just had meatloaf yesterday."

"Not *mine*," her mother said.

"I can't wait," Michael assured her. "I hope the sweet potatoes come with *Merry Little Marshmallows*."

Amber smiled. Mom would have that covered. Now, if only she had brought a little mistletoe for the meatloaf...

• • •

Michael secured his skis to the rack on top of the SUV. Across from him, Nick did the same.

When they had made arrangements yesterday, he hadn't planned to have so much company along for their day of skiing. A busy and, he had to admit, fun day. Too bad Amber had elected to stay at the lodge.

He looked around him. Christmas week in a tourist trap. And with all the fresh snow that had fallen in the past week or so, it made sense a crowd would hit the slopes. He had expected that crowd to be made up of tourists, along with plenty of the residents of Snowflake Valley. But who knew so many of the locals would all have the same last name.

"These Barnetts," he mumbled, "they like to operate by committee."

Nick laughed. "They sure do. All this family togetherness is going to take some getting used to, since I'm an only child."

Lucky you. He'd have traded that status with Nick in an instant.

He also hadn't expected to be the center of attention today. Word definitely got around in Snowflake Valley. Every local they'd encountered had heard about the mayor's nomination. If one more person came up to him…

Wouldn't Amber be calling him Scrooge now? She would have been gracious about the congratulations. Happy for the good wishes. And, no matter how she downplayed the Snow Ball nominations, she couldn't fool him. She was thrilled by the idea of being crowned Queen. She should have been here today. For her sake…

Or for his?

"Whoo—that was fun," said one of the twins as she jogged past him.

Mandy. Maybe. They both had the same blue eyes, the same long, curly red-brown hair, and at the moment, the same matching grins. Though he still couldn't tell them apart, he had finally learned their names—Mandy and Brooke. The boys were Josh and Drew.

"I need to get warm," the other twin said.

They raced toward the family van. Their dad and brothers followed more slowly.

After a last check of their skis, he and Nick climbed into the SUV.

Through the windshield, he watched the Barnetts piling into the van. "That man did a good job keeping up with his kids. I don't see how he managed, considering all their energy. The girls especially."

"Don't let the gray hairs fool you," Nick said. "He runs every day and plays racquetball three times a week. He's good with a basketball, too."

His dad had never done any of those things. He'd always been too busy working.

"Impressive." Both Mr. Barnett's accomplishments and Nick's knowledge of them. His friend had learned more about the Barnetts than he had. That made sense, as Nick and Lyssa had dated for a few months last summer, while he and Amber…

There was no *he and Amber.*

He should have remembered that yesterday, before he'd kissed her again. But like a kid in a Snowflake Valley toy store, he couldn't keep from reaching out for what he wanted.

"Are you with me?" Nick asked.

He started. "What?"

"The twins. All that energy, remember? The girls go non-stop. And from what I can see, Lyssa and Amber and Callie are the same. They all get it from their mom and dad."

"Then I hope they've all gotten those posters done."

"I don't think they expected help with that. But they'll have plenty of other stuff for us to do."

"*Us*? That had better mean you and the Barnetts."

Nick laughed. "Actually, old friend"—his tone made Michael grit his teeth—"Lyssa said they really needed the help, so I threw your name into the hat."

"Then take it out again."

"I can't do that. Callie already made you and Amber a team. You can't back out now. Besides, you can't tell me you haven't already committed to Amber."

"*What?*"

"What, *what*? Stay with me, man. Are you sure you're awake enough to drive?"

"I'm fine." Up ahead, the van had pulled out of the parking lot and onto the main road. He nosed the SUV after it.

Nick stared at him. "I'm saying you must have told Amber you're on board with this festival. But anyhow, remember last winter, when you needed someone to help you out and play Santa for the party at the lodge?"

"*Amber* requested help."

"Yeah. From *you*."

"So? I delegated authority."

"No, you asked for a favor. From *me*. Not once, but twice. I helped you out again this year. You owe me."

Just what he'd said to Amber. His first mistake. Luckily, last night's conversation had saved him from doing something stupid. Like kissing her again. It had helped him remember the reality of their so-called relationship. Amber wanted things he couldn't give her. A family. Kids. And a man who could be a good dad.

"I'm here for some R-and-R and time on the slopes," he told Nick. "Not to run around town picking up people's donations."

Or to gather more goodwill from the folks of Snowflake Valley…

The other man shrugged. "It's your call."

As he drove along the snow-packed roadway, he thought about Mrs. Barnett thanking him for buying lunch. Of Mr. Barnett, wanting him to try the family-secret recipe. And of Lyssa, who probably figured her fiancé's best friend would be more than happy to join the committee. And yes, he thought about his buddy willingly doing him those favors.

Finally, he gave up fighting the rest of his thoughts and let them to drift to Amber.

Amber, who didn't seem to think much of him at all.

Where's your heart? she had asked.

If you weren't such a Scrooge…

He swore under his breath. But no matter how he tried, he couldn't manage even a silent *Bah, humbug.*

• • •

They had done a good day's work. After Amber helped Callie and Lyssa clear off the dining room table, she went to check on Penny, asleep in the living room. Everyone else headed to the kitchen.

Or she thought they had, until she found she wasn't walking alone. One look at Lyssa's face told her something was up. "Did you think I'd get lost along the way?" she asked.

"No, I thought this might be a good chance for us to chat."

"We've been chatting all day."

"Very funny."

Penny was still sleeping soundly, her cheeks slightly pink and her lips pursed in a baby smile. Amber couldn't help smiling, too. She touched one of her daughter's curls, light brown and softer than a feather. She loved her daughter more than anything in life. That alone should keep her far away from any man who didn't want a family.

What did it say about her that she still wanted Michael?

"I'm glad everything's working out for you," Lyssa said.

If she only knew…

"And believe me," she continued, "I hope things get even better between you and Michael."

"I'm not—"

"You're not about to argue with me," Lyssa said with a smile. "That *is* what you were going to say, right? Because I've known all along how you feel about him. So has Callie."

She cringed. She thought she'd hidden those feelings so well. "It's that obvious?"

"No. Not to everyone. But we know you better than anyone else does."

Penny squirmed, bringing her tiny fist to her mouth. "That's definitely a sign she'll want to eat soon." Amber watched her for a minute. "Having Penny is the best thing that's ever happened to me." She turned to Lyssa. "Remember the last time I thought I had feelings for someone? Penny's the only good thing to come from that disaster."

"Everyone's entitled to mess up a few times until they get things right. That was your first serious relationship."

"First and only," she said bitterly. "And probably last."

"What about Michael?"

Why had she ever agreed to this pretend-dating relationship? The thought made her cringe again. Michael had come up with the plan to help her. "It's…not that serious yet." For him. "We're just taking things day-by-day. No guarantees. No promises." And once the week was over, no more pretending. "Don't be surprised if we don't last. I'll probably be a bad-luck Barnett sister for the rest of my life."

Lyssa smothered a laugh. "You're so dramatic sometimes, Amber. I can't believe Callie and I once had to talk you out of stage fright. You're *not* going to have bad luck forever. Not if you go after what you want."

She took the baby from the playpen. "Penny is all I want right now."

"Because you're afraid to look for more?"

"I *can't* look for more from Michael."

"It didn't seem like that yesterday when you were kissing beneath the mistletoe."

"Only because *you* wouldn't give up."

Now, Lyssa didn't bother trying to hide her laugh.

Amber pretended to scowl at her, but in her heart, she knew Lyssa was just looking out for her, as always. As they all did for each other. She loved growing up with so many sisters and brothers around, and she couldn't imagine her life without them—or without a large family of her own someday. But Michael…

The sounds of raised voices and laughter came from the kitchen.

"Everyone must be back from skiing."

"Great. Then Michael will get the good news Callie teamed you up with him. We'll see what happens when you two are running around town together picking up donations."

She laughed. "Don't have your heart set on anything regarding Michael." Good advice *her* heart needed to follow, too. "We won't be running around together."

"But you're running for King and Queen."

"That's different." A means to an end for Michael. That didn't matter, as long as the competition led to the contract he needed. If nothing else, she had to get through the rest of this week for him. "The auction's a family project. *Our* family project. And trust me, he doesn't want anything to do with it." She glanced down at Penny. "Come on, I need to feed this little girl."

In the kitchen, the skiers were stripping off mittens, jackets, and hats.

Michael stood near the table. He pulled off his cap, ruffling his hair. His face looked relaxed. Happy. So different from his blank expression that morning.

His easy smile made her warm all over.

Wasn't she stronger than this? With her face flushing from a heat wave, how could she keep him from realizing how she felt? She leaned over to give Penny another kiss.

Without looking, she knew the moment Michael crossed the room to stand beside her. Reluctantly, she raised her head.

"Hey, partner," he said. "I hear we're a team."

• • •

Michael had agreed truthfully that Mrs. Barnett's meatloaf was even better than what he'd eaten at the Candy Cane. He didn't have a word of complaint about the three kinds of desserts, either.

One of the twins sat back in her chair and sighed heavily. Mandy, he felt sure, only because someone had said her name earlier and the twins hadn't moved from the table since. "I'm stuffed," she announced.

"You oughta be," Josh said. "You ate enough for three people."

"You oughta know," she shot back, "since you do that all the time."

Drew jumped to his brother's defense. "Why wouldn't he? He's finally got the chance, now that you and Brooke are out of the house for a while."

"And *that's* exactly why Mandy and I decided to go to away to school," Brooke said. "To get away from both of *you*."

Everyone laughed. Definitely not the way a conversation like that would have gone at his dad's house.

Once the table was cleared and the dishes done and put away, the teams were given their routes for the donation pickups. At that point, Mr. Barnett announced it was time to go home.

"Are you coming back to the house for a while, Amber?"

Mrs. Barnett asked.

He could sense Amber's struggle to keep from looking at him. "Not tonight, Mom. I've got a few things to finish up here. Then I plan to get to bed early and hope Penny makes it through most of the night. And…and Michael and I probably should get an early start tomorrow."

"No probably about that," he said. "We need to get a jump on those pickups. I think you and I drew the short straw for the longest list."

Everyone laughed and, as he had hoped, her family's attention shifted from Amber. Still talking, they moved off to gather up their jackets and hats.

Finally, the front door closed behind Nick and the Barnetts, and he was left alone with Amber and her daughter. She settled Penny in the playpen, then took a seat on the couch. Light came only from the fixture over the dining room table, the Christmas tree, and the fireplace. Amber stared at the flames.

Without a word, he took the chair beside the couch, content just to watch her. She was still, and yet she wasn't. Flickering light from the fire danced across her, giving the illusion of movement. From the corner of the room, the Christmas tree lights blinked, reflecting in her hair.

After a while, she glanced at him. "Thanks for the save. About the early start for our morning, I mean."

"That wasn't a save. I meant it. The team with the most donations wins, right?"

She laughed, her eyes suddenly gleaming. "No, that's not right. Sorry. We don't compete with one another. Well, except on game nights."

"The Super Bowl? The World Series?"

"Monopoly and dominoes."

He shook his head. "You guys are too good to be true. Do you dress up to pose for Christmas photos together, too?"

Wrong move. The brightness left her eyes. Her shoulders stiffened.

He had to remember not everyone had a family like his. Especially not Amber.

"Yes, we do take group pictures. What's wrong with that?"

"Nothing, I guess. It's just not something we do in my family."

"What *do* you do?"

"As I said the other day, we go our separate ways."

"And as I said, that's sad."

"No, it's just the way things are."

"Why?"

"I don't know. It's hard to explain." And would mean having a conversation he didn't want to get into. But she would keep asking because she was Amber and she was all about family. If not tonight or this week, she would ask this question again when he made another trip to the lodge. "Not everybody's got the picture-perfect family."

"*Nobody* has that, whether they take group photos or not."

"Yeah, well. Some are less perfect than others." She opened her mouth, but he shook his head. "Don't ask. It's too complicated to get into."

He could see concern in her eyes and almost hear the rest of her questions. But after a moment, she turned away.

"I should get Penny upstairs."

I should get you *upstairs.*

The thought hit without warning, and his body's instant response showed just how well he liked the idea. But his brain knew there was more to his interest in Amber than getting her into bed.

Again, he watched the reflections dance over her. He wished he were sitting beside her, running his fingers down her hair, trying to catch the twinkling Christmas lights.

That was it.

That was what he'd always found different about her. What she had brought into his life from the day he had met her. Her sparkling eyes. Her sunny smile. Her light. They kept his thoughts coming back to her no matter how hard he fought them, no matter how many times he reminded himself she was off-limits. He'd forgotten or pushed away or just plain ignored those reminders. Instead, he needed to listen to them. Starting now.

He shot to his feet as she rose from the couch.

She froze, looking up at him uncertainly. But she didn't back away. She didn't look away. Those sparkling eyes of hers stared into his, drawing him to her. Instead of backing up and walking off the way he'd intended to—the way he should have—he stepped forward, as if he had no choice in the matter. And maybe he hadn't.

Maybe there was a reason he had come to the lodge just when Amber had decided to hide out here.

Maybe he wasn't meant to keep his thoughts away from her.

Or his hands off her.

He trailed his fingertips along her jaw, then lifted her chin. Her eyes widened and her lips parted and her breath exhaled in a rush that halted any thought he'd had of walking away.

With the tip of his thumb, he grazed her bottom lip. Her answering indrawn breath made it impossible for him to keep from lowering his mouth to hers.

One more taste…

But even as his lips brushed hers, he knew that taste would come with a price he wouldn't want to pay.

Chapter Ten

Amber let her eyes drift closed, wanting to focus the rest of her senses on this moment, needing to savor the taste and texture and pressure of Michael's mouth on hers. He cradled her face in his hands, sending a tingle of pleasure through her, a shivery little show of proof that this could be so right…

Then why did something feel all wrong?

Her first clue came with Michael's sigh.

She opened her eyes to find his gaze meeting hers. His eyes were dark and shadowed. Now she wished she hadn't turned off the table lamps. She wished he would look toward the fire so she could read his expression.

His fingertips skimmed her cheeks, his touch oh so gentle. Another clue. He was treating her like something easily broken. Without saying a word, he was letting her go.

Well, she wouldn't break. Those days were over. And she wouldn't go quietly. "What is it?"

He sighed. "Pretending in front of your family is fine with me. But alone with you, I can't pretend. I can't lie. I want you."

Her breath caught in her throat, leaving her struggling to speak, let alone breathe. "Michael," she managed to whisper, "you have to know I want you, too."

Backing up a step, he shoved his hands into his back pockets, as if to keep from touching her. "The difference is, I don't *want* to want you."

His words, his actions, his body language, all said he was fighting as hard as she was. The thought brought on another shiver of pleasure and allowed her a glimmer of hope. Struggle meant he was coming a step closer to her, maybe rethinking his ideas and even changing his mind about the holidays…and more.

He ran his hand through his hair and sighed again. But he didn't break eye contact. Another glimmer of hope. "I don't want to hurt you."

"What makes you think you will?"

"Every conversation we've had about family."

"I need more of an explanation than that. As you said to me once before, you owe me."

He winced. "All right. One example. Tonight, when the kids were all going at each other at the supper table. Everyone ended up laughing. You wouldn't see that in my family. The teasing would turn ugly. Somebody would knock a glass or three onto the floor. Somebody else would throw a few punches."

"You're a family of boys. You play rougher."

"No. We're a family of mutts, from two different moms and four different dads."

"That doesn't mean you can never have a family of your own."

"And that's where I'll hurt you," he said quietly. "You believe in family. I don't."

She'd been wrong. She *would* break. But not in front of Michael. She took a steadying breath and let it out slowly.

"What now? Are you firing me?"

"Of course not." He sounded shocked.

"Then we'll keep doing what we've been doing, until we get through the week. Pretending in front of my family and everyone else. Helping out with the auction. Running for King and Queen." She could feel her heart crumbling to pieces as she spoke.

"You want to be Queen of the Ball, don't you?"

"I want you to get that contract."

"I can't ask you to help me with that."

"You're not asking. I volunteered. Besides, it's for the greater good of Snowflake Valley, isn't it?"

He nodded.

"But this can't happen again. No more kisses. At least, not when we're alone."

"You're right."

For the first time in her life, she wanted to be wrong. "We'd better say good night. We have an early start in the morning and a long day ahead." For a moment, she hesitated, her determination weakening. Before she could make the mistake of stepping forward, of reaching for him, he turned away and went to take care of the fire.

Exhaling half in relief, half in disappointment, she crossed to the Christmas tree and turned off the lights.

After Michael said good night, she stood in the shadowy corner of the living room, watching until he had gone up the stairs and disappeared from her sight. She wanted to call after him, to run after him, to tell him this agreement wasn't going to work. It wasn't enough.

Instead, she went to cuddle her daughter. Penny squirmed slightly in her arms. "Don't worry, sweetie-pie," she murmured, "Mommy's got you. And she's not going anywhere. Not even upstairs to chase after Michael."

Penny let out a little whimpering cry.

"I know," she whispered. "Mommy's not happy about that, either."

• • •

Before the morning was half done, Michael had burned up a tank of gas. Working through their list of homeowners donating to the auction had netted them so many items, they'd had to make several trips to the elementary school to unload the SUV.

Somehow, he and Amber had managed to act as though they hadn't had their conversation last night. Act being the key word.

Close to noon, he added the current contribution to the SUV, then made his way back up the path toward the house. Amber stood on the front porch with the elderly homeowner, a woman so tiny, one blast of the backdraft from Santa's sleigh would probably topple her.

"Thank you again, Mrs. Anderson," Amber said. "We really appreciate your generosity."

"My pleasure, always." The woman rested her hand on Amber's arm. "And don't you worry a bit about the ball, dear. You know any Barnett will get my vote."

He smiled. How many times had someone told them that this morning? Like many of those others, Mrs. Anderson continued, "I'll be sure to vote for your young man, too." She glanced toward him and added something new. "He'll make a handsome King, won't he?"

Amber smiled. "A very handsome one."

He gave her a small bow. "With a very beautiful Queen by his side."

Mrs. Anderson giggled, and Amber's cheeks turned pink.

As they climbed into the SUV, he said, "We've got

another full load. Is this why you all waited a couple of days after Christmas to collect the loot? Is everyone getting rid of their surplus now that Santa's brought them their new gifts?"

"No. We're just a giving bunch here in Snowflake Valley."

He wished she would give him the same sunny smile she'd sent him a minute ago. "You doing okay?"

"I'm fighting a headache."

He pulled to a stop at a light on the main street, Icicle Lane—what else?—and looked over at her again. She wore a fuzzy blue hat patterned with white snowflakes that brought out the blue in her eyes. It also accentuated the strained look around them. "You told me you hadn't been feeling well on Christmas Eve. Do you think you're still coming down with something?"

"No. I'm fine. I'm probably just tired more than anything."

"Did Penny keep you up again last night?"

"She's a baby," she snapped. "She cries."

"I know babies cry. I heard enough of that when I was a kid. I asked if Penny kept you up because I can see by your face that you're worn out."

"And short-tempered, obviously," she murmured. "It's just a headache. I'm sorry for snapping."

She didn't sound overly sorry. He gripped the steering wheel, trying not to beat himself up for what he had told her last night. Trying not to believe he was to blame for her lack of sleep. She'd already known he didn't want a family.

For the next few blocks, they rode in silence.

The SUV bumped over packed snow near the entrance to the school's rear driveway. Slowing to a crawl, he crossed the parking lot and pulled as close as he could to the back doors of the two-storied redbrick building. "Is this where you went to school?"

She nodded. "We all did. Penny will come here, too."

"I can picture you in grade school," he told her. "I'll bet

you were a good student."

"You're half right." A reluctant smile tugged at her lips. "I loved the first year. But after I graduated and moved up from kindergarten into elementary, I tried to skate by in class. Who wants to do all that studying? Luckily, as I told you, I had Callie and Lyssa and their tutoring sessions. They got me through."

There she went again—giving others credit for an accomplishment she must have worked hard at, too. "I'm sure you buckled down when necessary."

That brought a laugh. "I didn't have a choice. Even way back then, Callie was a born teacher. She had a way of tricking me into paying attention, especially when I didn't want to."

A good talent to have. Not that he needed the skill, considering when it came to Amber, he needed to keep his distance.

The door of the school opened. Callie stepped out onto the concrete step spanning the width of the building. Josh and Drew followed. "She's still carrying that clipboard. I haven't seen her without it once this morning."

"She lives by clipboards and calendars and spreadsheets and lesson plans. She's the most organized person I've ever known."

"Are you always so complimentary about your family?"

Her eyebrows rose in surprise. "I'm not complimenting her, just telling you what she's like."

She focused on positives and strengths, the same qualities he tried to highlight in performance reviews with his employees. *That's* what he should be noticing about Amber—her willingness to work and her ability to get a job done. He needed to forget about her sparkling blue eyes and bright smile and the taste of her lips.

They climbed out of the SUV to meet Callie. The two boys veered toward the back of the vehicle to begin unloading boxes. Michael joined them, leaving Amber to bring her sister up to speed on their latest trip.

The older boy, Josh, gave an admiring whistle. "You made an even bigger haul this time than you did the last."

"Yeah." Drew laughed. "You'd better not let Callie see this. She'll put you on her volunteer list for the rest of your life."

He tried to envision a lifetime spent working with the Barnetts…

"You going to be around for the New Year's Eve party?" Drew asked.

"Of course he will, dude," Josh said. "He's running for Snow Ball King."

"That's correct," he agreed. "Besides, I wouldn't want to miss seeing the New Year arrive here in Snowflake Valley, would I?" To his surprise, the idea didn't sound half-bad. "But if you two don't get this vehicle unloaded, I won't get credit for the haul, and Callie might have me struck from the ballot."

"We'll get right to it," Josh said.

Drew nodded agreement.

Smiling, Michael went back to Amber and Callie, who stood with their heads together over Callie's clipboard. "You've got those two men well-trained," he said to her.

"Years of experience."

"With fourth-graders," Amber added.

"Hey!" Drew yelled. "We heard that. Are you comparing us to elementary-school kids?"

"You're not that evolved," Callie called back.

"Fine. Then I'm ready for my milk and cookies."

"You're in luck. It's almost time for lunch." She turned back to Michael and Amber. "You two are included in the invitation. How far did you get with the pickups?"

"About halfway," Amber said. "Down the list, not

geographically. We'll probably have a few stops tomorrow, too."

Callie looked at him again. "I hope Amber told you to keep track of mileage. We'll reimburse you for expenses."

Nice. In his family, he'd be the one handing over the cash. But he shook his head. "No need. Consider it my donation to the cause."

"Thanks." Callie smiled. She and Amber headed toward the school. For a minute, he stayed where he was, watching them.

Both sisters had long, wavy hair. Callie's was a reddish-brown. Amber's hair in the sunshine looked like dark liquid gold.

Under his breath, he swore to himself. What a fool. Liquid gold and sparkling blue. At this rate, he could fire the people who took care of advertising for the company and write the copy himself.

He caught up to them in Callie's classroom. Before they broke for lunch, she had them tag everything that had been collected so far. She ran down the list he and Amber had followed, logging each item into the computer, then printing a descriptive card to go with it.

"That's it!" Mandy took the final card and tagged it to its matching item. "Aren't you thrilled to have so many happy helpers?"

She had spoken in a teasing tone, but Callie answered seriously, "I couldn't have done this job without all of you."

"Including Michael?" Brooke asked, shooting him a glance.

"Most especially Michael."

"Yeah, sure," he said, laughing.

"In fact," Callie said, "I think I'll elevate Michael to my second-in-command."

She didn't mean it. Still, the statement made him feel part

of the team. Part of the…family.

How did he handle that? Would it have made a difference if the compliment had come from Amber? “Thanks, but I’ll pass on the promotion. There are too many Barnetts in line ahead of me. And don’t forget Nick.”

“Forget me,” Nick pleaded. “Please, forget me.”

As everyone laughed, Lyssa wrapped her arms around him and gave him a loud, smacking kiss. “Oh, no, sweetheart, we have *big* plans for you.”

“We sure do,” Callie confirmed.

Suddenly Michael envied the man he had pitied just days ago.

Chapter Eleven

The setting sun left the lodge's kitchen in deep shadows. Amber flipped on the overhead lights, then wished she hadn't. One look at her reflection in the window over the sink made her wince.

Michael was right. She did look tired. The long day didn't help, especially when she'd spent most of it thinking of him… and his kisses.

And those thoughts wouldn't bring her anything but another endless night of heartache. In the glass, she watched the image of her fingertips brushing across her mouth, as if she could brush away the memory of his lips on hers.

The back door swung open. Michael entered the kitchen, bringing in a swirl of cold air with him. He set a couple of grocery sacks on the counter. "This is the last of them. It's a good thing we got to the store when we did. It looked like everyone else in town had already raided the place."

"It's a holiday week," she said automatically.

He laughed. "It's always a holiday here, isn't it?"

To her surprise, he sounded less critical than usual. Still, it made her sad to know he couldn't resist another jab at her beloved hometown.

"I'm going to bring in some firewood from the garage."

When he left, the room seemed colder by another few degrees. Just her imagination. The temperature in the kitchen hadn't fallen, but her mood at watching him go through the door sure had dropped.

Being near him made her feel warm and secure and...

Unhappy.

All during lunch, she had held her breath, hoping no one in her family would invite them for supper at home or suggest going out to eat again. She had finally had enough of family togetherness—at least for now, when her resistance to Michael was weakening by the second.

The telephone rang, startling her. Penny cried out.

"Shh, baby," she called as she grabbed the receiver. "It's only the phone. Hello?"

"Hey, this is Derek. Is Mike around?"

She frowned. *Funny.* She had never heard anyone call her boss anything but Michael. "Not right at the moment, but he'll be back in a few minutes. Can I take a message?"

"Nah. I'll call him again sometime. I'm his brother."

His *brother.* She had never had the opportunity to talk to anyone in Michael's family. "I'm Amber. His housekeeper. I'll tell him you called. I know he'll be sorry he missed you."

"He'll be sorry, all right," the man said with an odd laugh. "So, he's planning to be at the lodge for a while, huh?"

"At least for the rest of the week. It's a good time for him to stay, since we'll be celebrating our Winter Festival here in Snowflake Valley."

"Yeah? What's that all about?"

He seemed genuinely interested, and she was always ready to share the highlights of her hometown. She ran enthusiastically down the list of scheduled events—the ice-skating pageant, the bobsled races, the Christmas campfire, and so much more.

"Sounds like a real fun time," Derek said dryly.

His change in tone surprised her. "It will be fun," she replied, trying not to go on the defensive. She'd done that when Michael had talked about her family's holiday photos. This man was part of *Michael's* family. "It's always a fun time," she went on, hoping to win him over to the joys of living in the valley. Maybe if one of the DeFrancos believed, a second would follow…

"Yeah, well," he said, "I'll try to reach Mike some other time. Don't bother telling him I called. We'll let it be a surprise when I get in touch." He gave that odd laugh again, then hung up.

Frowning, she replaced the receiver. She had barely turned back to the groceries when the door swung open again and Michael entered, carrying an armload of logs.

With a glance at Penny, who now lay sleeping in her carrier on the kitchen table, he set the logs quietly into the wooden box beside the door. He sat on the bench to remove his snow-covered boots. "Man, it's cold out there."

"They're predicting another storm," she told him.

"I heard that on the radio. That's another thing I would think you'd get tired of in this town, except when you want to ski. Not a lot of alternatives. Snow and bad weather, bad weather and snow."

"You can have bad weather anywhere. And the snow is beautiful when it first falls."

"Like a Christmas card." His laugh sounded strained, reminding her of Derek's. Why did she feel she should ignore the man's request and tell Michael his brother had called?

He gathered up the armload of logs. "I'm going to start a fire. Maybe it'll keep the lodge so warm, the snow will melt as soon as it hits."

Scrooge, she thought but didn't say. She watched him walk out the door.

He would come around to her way of thinking. Soon.

Again, she thought of telling him about his brother's call. Maybe hearing someone in his family cared about getting in touch would make him feel better about them.

Or maybe that wasn't such a good idea. She really had almost gone overboard about the Winter Festival. She imagined Michael's reaction to that conversation. Definitely not good. It was probably best just to follow Derek's request and say nothing at all.

Why keep rocking the boat? Why make trouble, when she had so few days left with Michael? She planned to show off Snowflake Valley to him during the festival. She planned to show *him* off, too, in town and at the Snow Ball.

I don't want *to want you.*

But oh, she wanted him. Until he left, she was determined to spend as much time with him as she could. And more…

She wanted him to *want* to spend his free time with her and Penny.

• • •

They made salmon, rice, and asparagus for supper. Michael volunteered to handle the lemon and dill salmon in the broiler. Amber looked like she might turn down the offer, but finally said she would take care of the side dishes.

After supper, she closed the dishwasher door with a bang. "That's it," she said. "I'm running it tonight instead of waiting until the morning."

"Sounds good."

And they sounded like an old married couple sharing a nightly ritual. Once, the thought of falling into a rut like that would have made him run for the hills. Now, it gave him a sense of closeness to her.

He didn't want the *sense* of it, he wanted the actuality. But after last night's conversation—and last night's kiss—he knew better than to try to get near her again.

She carried Penny out of the kitchen into the living room. Through the slice of doorway that he could see from his seat at the table, he eyed them both snuggling together on the couch. Trying not to think about snuggling with Amber himself, he turned to the laptop he had left on the kitchen counter.

After an hour of scrolling through computer files and seeing nothing on the screen, he gave up. And gave in. He raided the kitchen pantry and the cabinet near the sink.

When he walked into the living room carrying the long-handled pot he'd found, Amber looked up from the book she had been reading. Her eyes widened. "What's that?"

"Looks like a saucepan to me."

"And what are you planning to do with it?"

He held out the bottle of cooking oil he'd gotten from the pantry. "Make some popcorn. Any problem with that idea?"

She shook her head. "Nope. As long as we add *lots* of butter. That is, if you're planning to eat it and not string it up to decorate the Christmas tree." She raised her brows.

"Yeah, I'm planning to eat it. But I didn't bring any butter."

"I'll get some."

"Sounds good."

There they went again, with that old-married-couple conversation. He took it as an encouraging sign.

He readied the pan and held it over the fire, heating the oil. Amber returned with a chunk of butter on a plate and one big bowl for them to share.

She curled up on the end of the couch closest to him. "The salmon you made was great. I thought you said cooking from scratch wasn't on your resume."

"Shoving something under the broiler isn't really much of a stretch."

"For some people it is. So, where did you learn to cook? Boy Scouts?"

He shook his head. "No. I was never a Scout. I learned out of self-preservation after Mama died."

"Your grandmother," she clarified.

"Yeah."

"Didn't your stepmom cook?"

He gripped the handle of the pot. She sat there watching him, waiting for him to answer. Instead, he shook the pot over the fire. Corn kernels began pinging like buckshot against the lid.

She couldn't have known her innocent question would bring back memories he didn't want to have. Or would lead the conversation in a direction he didn't want to go.

Chapter Twelve

The living room filled with the scent and sound of popping corn. Over the noise, Amber waited. Having Michael answer her question suddenly meant more to her than the answer itself.

He came to sit beside her on the couch. She moved a stack of magazines on the coffee table. When he set the pot on top of them, she added the butter to the hot popcorn and waited some more.

"My stepmother didn't do much of anything if she could help it," he said finally. "At least, not when my dad was working."

"And when he was around..."

"Which wasn't often." He shrugged. "She lucked into a good situation by marrying my dad. When he was around, she made things look good. When he was off at work...well, my grandmother was born to take care of a family. Mama DeFranco had already been running the kitchen and the rest of the house for so long, ever since my mom died. When my dad remarried, she just kept doing what she had always done."

"Taking care of you and him," she said softly.

"And then later, everyone else."

"You said she passed away when you were nine."

"Yeah."

"How old were you when your mother died?"

"Four."

Her eyes blurred from sudden tears. She thought of Michael at that age. She thought of leaving Penny and never seeing her grow up. "You were so young to lose her."

"She was so young to go."

"I'm sorry."

"It was a long time ago. I don't think of her that often."

She could see in his face that he was thinking of his mother now, that he hadn't forgotten her, that he never would. Her heart hurt for him. He'd had to deal with that loss, and then to face having a woman come into his life who apparently hadn't even tried to fill the gap.

"You mentioned brothers," she said tentatively.

To her disappointment, he didn't answer. Grabbing the spoon she had brought from the kitchen, she stirred the popcorn, and transferred it into the bowl. And waited.

Finally, he said, "That'll be getting cold." He reached for the bowl and set it onto his lap.

She would need to scoot closer to him to be within reaching distance of her snack. Maybe he had planned it that way.

And maybe she spent too much time in wishful thinking. After all, he hadn't made a move toward her since he had kissed her in this very room last night.

Why not drown her sorrows in popcorn? She took a handful, loving the buttery slickness and the sting of salt. She ran her tongue across her bottom lip and dug in to the bowl again. When she looked up, Michael sat staring at her.

Swallowing hard, she almost choked on an unpopped kernel. He leaned over to brush his mouth against hers. She responded eagerly, automatically, liking the burst of buttery, salty flavor on his lips even more than she had on her own.

He tucked his fingers beneath her chin, tilting her face up as though he wanted to kiss her—to taste her—more thoroughly. And oh, she wanted that, too.

But she'd shared kisses and more in a relationship that had gone wrong. She couldn't risk that now. With Michael, she wanted everything to go right.

She sat back, shaking her head. "We agreed this wouldn't happen again."

His smile turned her insides softer than heated butter. The feeling was almost—but not quite—enough to make her forget he didn't like family and kids and Christmas.

"What do you mean, 'happen again?'" he asked. "This is the first time we've ever shared a bowl of popcorn. At least, as far as I can remember."

He was teasing her, and she was certainly used to that from her brothers and sisters. But this was different. Much different. "I'm not talking about the popcorn, Michael."

"Yeah, I know."

"Sharing a snack and...and any other things might be fun for the moment. But we don't share enough—of life in general—to make this anything permanent. And I'll confess," she said reluctantly, her cheeks heating, "right this minute, doing the right thing is hard enough for me. Don't make it any harder."

"You think it's easy for me?"

Her heart gave an erratic jump. Maybe she meant more to him—

No. Don't go there. He'd already told her just how he felt. Wishing wouldn't change things. A miracle might. But until that happened...

She grabbed the bowl and held it out to him. "Let's just stick to our agreement. And our snack."

• • •

Michael shook hands with the man standing beside the skating rink, then patted his toddler son's head. Nothing to it. Just as Mayor Corrigan had said.

"You think you have a chance at winning King of the Snow Ball?" the man asked.

He shrugged. "I don't know about me, but Amber's a sure win for Queen." He draped his arm around her and admired her cheeks, pink either from the cold or his compliment. Only one way to find out. And here they were, out in public—the perfect place to uphold their agreement. He kissed her cheek. Sure enough, the pale pink became a rosy glow.

"Thanks," she said. "I'll do my best, too."

The man headed to the concession stands.

Michael gestured around them. "We're not alone, that's for sure." He took a seat on a nearby wooden bench and grunted in satisfaction as he leaned down to tie the laces on his skate.

After more donation pickups that morning and another brown-bag lunch in her classroom, Callie had announced they had the rest of the day off. The entire group of Barnett siblings convened a meeting to decide what they would do with their free time. He had never seen such an organized bunch—but he had to admit they'd been on the mark about this afternoon. Not ten minutes yet, and being here at the skating rink had already gotten him more than a few handshakes and promises of support for the ball.

And it was going to get him closer to Amber.

Bending down for the second skate, he gave another grunt of satisfaction.

"Need help with those laces?" she asked mildly.

He caught the glint of mischief in her eyes. Just like with the snowball fight, she thought she was up against a rookie.

She had no idea he'd made a sacrifice play, letting her win. Why not, when their kiss in the snow meant he'd taken the trophy. "Think I can handle it, thanks. Seven years of ice hockey gives you plenty of practice putting on your skates."

Her eyes widened.

"All right, let's go." He stood and pulled her to her feet. "Show me your stuff."

She started across the ice at an easy pace, then picked up speed as they moved into the middle of the rink. He matched her glide for glide. For good measure—and his own pleasure—he slipped his arm around her waist. He took her free hand in his and held it against his chest. "Looks like you've done a few turns on the ice, too. What position did you play?"

"Very funny. Ice hockey wasn't my thing."

"Let me guess. Figure skating. And you sure have the—"

"*Hush*," she said, but he heard the laughter in her tone. "I never did that, either. But I know where you're going with the line, and trust me, I've heard it a million times before."

"Guess I'll have to try for something more original, then."

"Or quit while you're ahead."

"No fun in that."

Her brothers suddenly came up on either side of them. They expertly glided backward into the space ahead of him and Amber, but far enough away to give them all enough room to skate. "Not bad," he said with a nod.

"We're naturals." Josh laughed. "Too bad Amber doesn't have our skating genes."

"Yeah," Drew said. "We wanted to warn you, you're taking a real chance with her."

"You're a good man, Michael," Josh told him, "and we'd hate to lose you in an unfortunate accident."

They were joking, he knew, and still their pretended concern about his safety felt good. "Thanks. I'll keep my eyes open." But maybe not his hands in place.

When the boys skated off, he smiled down at Amber. The sun glinted off her golden-brown hair and made her eyes sparkle. His breath caught in his chest.

She rolled those beautiful eyes. "Everybody's a comedian," she said grimly.

"They're just watching out for you."

"Please. That show of male solidarity was them looking out for *you*."

Male solidarity. Something he'd never experienced with his own brothers. Funny that he should get an offer of it from hers.

In front of them, a snow-suited little girl took a tumble. Holding Amber's waist more firmly, he swung her to arm's length in front of him, moving her wide of the girl, who sprawled on the ice, laughing. Amber frowned. With the way she felt about kids, she'd be concerned.

As they sailed on, he looked over his shoulder. "No worries. Someone already helped her up. She's skating again. But she'll be hurting tomorrow," he predicted.

"It always hurts worse once you have time to sit and think about it."

He didn't understand her tone but knew he didn't like the sound of it. Resettling his arm around her waist, he leaned close and said, "I'd rather think about impressing you again."

"Who said you did that a first time?"

"Now, that sounds like a challenge." He glanced over his shoulder, looked forward, spotted a break in the stream of skaters. He raced toward the opening, sweeping Amber along beside him. Then he skated around the rink, tracing the oval again and again, always ready for the chance to power up his speed. After a while, Amber was laughing and gasping from the effort of keeping up with him. He'd gotten short of breath himself. But not from the exercise.

He angled across a free area to bring them away from the stream of skaters. When they reached the edge of the rink, he deposited her on a bench and stood in front of her. "Now tell me that didn't knock your socks right off."

"How could it?" she returned. "I'm not wearing socks."

No. She wore a pair of snug red tights that matched her flippy little skirt. His hands itched to go where they definitely shouldn't, especially not with most of her family and a rink full of people looking on. Instead, he dropped onto the bench beside her and took her hand in his again. He grasped the cuff of her glove and tugged, turning it inside out as he stripped it off her.

Her eyebrows rose. "My hand will get cold."

"Not if I keep it warm." He kissed her palm.

"What are you doing?" she demanded, the last word cracking in the middle.

"I just told you. Keeping your hand warm."

"I said it *will* get cold. It's not there yet."

"No problem. I can wait. Meanwhile, got any place else that's ready for attention?"

She shivered visibly. Probably from sitting on the concrete bench in only that short skirt and tights. But he wanted to believe something else had brought about her reaction. "Looks like *you're* cold now."

"Nothing a cup of hot chocolate won't cure."

"We can do that." Smiling, he leaned closer. "Or we can do something else and save the chocolate for a chaser." It was well past time for a mouth-to-mouth kiss. The look in her eyes told him she thought so, too. He leaned even closer.

Suddenly, that message in her eyes changed.

She rose to her feet and returned to the ice. As she powered away from him, her legs flashing, her hair flying, her skirt flipping around her hips, he was the one left shivering on the concrete bench.

Chapter Thirteen

Michael watched Amber disappear into the crowd. He could have followed her, would easily have caught up. But she had run off because he was ready to kiss her. She had liked the idea at first—he'd swear to that. Then she'd abruptly changed her mind.

Holding her on the ice had given him ideas he shouldn't have had. Had made him think about things he shouldn't want but did.

No, he had to stop kidding himself. He had wanted her long before he'd tied on his skates today.

Callie crossed the ice toward him, raising her hand in salute. She dropped onto the bench where Amber had been sitting.

Normally he'd have no problem with hanging out with one of the Barnetts. But right now, he had a feeling Amber's big sister had something on her mind. Something that—like Amber's abrupt departure—he wouldn't like at all.

"You're good at keeping secrets, aren't you?" she demanded.

Nothing like moving right in for the kill. Had Amber's family figured out the two of them weren't really a couple? That would be too ironic, to get found out now…just when their pretend relationship was starting to feel real to him.

"You were holding out on us," Callie continued. "You're a ringer in the rink."

He laughed. "Yeah, I've had some experience."

"We could see that. We could also see you and Amber looked good out there together."

"She's got better skating genes than your brothers seem to think."

"Don't let them fool you. We all grew up on the ice and the slopes. Amber included. The boys were teasing you because they like you. We all like you."

That comment pleased him more than it should have. "Well, thanks. The feeling's mutual."

"You're a good influence on Josh and Drew," she said.

"*Me?*"

"Yes. You and Nick. My dad's great with the boys, and they have plenty of male friends. But I think growing up in a houseful of girls made them always feel outnumbered."

That wasn't a feeling reserved for males growing up around females. You could feel outnumbered—even invisible—in a houseful of boys. He didn't like the memories this conversation was raising, just as he hadn't liked the question Amber had asked about his family last night. Instead of answering, he had taken advantage of the chance to get close to her. He'd done the same thing just now.

And he'd do it again in a heartbeat. Every time.

He glanced out over the stream of skaters. Plenty of red flashes to choose from, but none came from leggings and a flippy skirt. Where had she gone off to?

"You'll need a better attention span if you want to keep up with the Barnetts," Callie said lightly.

He started. "What?"

"You're daydreaming. For a minute, you looked just like one of my students."

"How can that be?" he said, forcing a grin. "I'll bet not one of them would zone out during your classes."

She laughed. "Oh, you're good. Flattery will get you far. It will even get me to tell you where Amber is. I saw her with Lyssa, headed to the concession stand, probably for a hot drink."

Nothing a cup of hot chocolate won't cure.

Amber had definitely gotten that wrong. Hot chocolate wouldn't come close to curing his need to get near her. At this point, most likely nothing could.

Callie sat eyeing him. She was sharp, and he'd messed up, zoning out again instead of responding. He should have claimed he wasn't wondering where Amber had gone.

Too late now. And judging by Callie's slow smile as she stood to return to the rink, she wouldn't have believed his protest, anyhow.

He couldn't complain that Callie had learned that much about him already.

Over the past few days, Amber's family seemed to have taken him under their collective wing. They made him feel more comfortable with them than he'd ever have thought possible. They gave him a feeling of belonging, of connection to their family that he had never found with his own. No, he had nothing to complain about.

Except the fact that he hadn't forged the same bonds with Amber.

• • •

Amber paced across the dining area and back again to the couch. How many times had she done this today? Worse, how many times had she looked over at Michael's closed office door?

Their afternoon at the skating rink had ended in a unanimous vote for supper from the concession stand. Hamburgers. And, for her, another hot chocolate. Every sip of her drink reminded her of Michael's suggestion to have a kiss first, and chocolate after.

She hadn't taken him up on the offer. What a waste.

Though they did have a good time feeding each other French fries…

She turned to pace back toward the couch and found him standing in the middle of the living room. Stumbling to a halt, she stared at him.

He had changed into a dark gray T-shirt that fit like a second skin. Black sweatpants rested low on his hips and skimmed the tops of his bare feet. In the light from the doorway behind him, his hair looked blue-black and tousled, as if he'd just woken up.

"Were you sleeping?" she asked.

"No. Doing some paperwork."

That again. Why the sudden attraction to work lately? Or… Wait. Could he be using that to help him forget his attraction to *her*? Because there was no denying, their time at the skating rink today proved he was interested.

And here she stood nearly drooling because he looked hot enough to melt the entire rink. *Think.* "I…uh…was going into the kitchen to make a cup of tea."

"Kitchen's that way." He gestured past her. Then he glanced at the novel she had left on the coffee table. "How's your book?"

"Fine." At least, it had received lots of great reviews. The entire time he had been in his office, she had sat on the couch with the book in her lap. On occasion, she had even remembered to turn an unread page.

"Guess I was rude to disappear for so long. Maybe I can make it up to you." He took a step toward her.

She curled her trembling fingers against her palms.

He took another step.

She thought about backing away, about telling him in no uncertain terms they *could not* get close to one another again. But did she have the acting skill to say it convincingly? Or the willpower to say it at all? She *wanted* to get close to Michael, even if she felt more stage fright right now than on the day of her kindergarten graduation. Even if it went against the terms of their agreement.

Because they were alone again, weren't they? Maybe she should point that out?

He took another step, and her pulse spiked. "You're not much of a reader, are you?" she blurted.

"No. I don't do a lot of reading. Of books, that is." He slanted a look toward the coffee table, then back to her. "From what I can see, you don't read much, either. It doesn't look like that bookmark has moved in days."

Busted. "There are reasons for that this week."

"Reasons?"

"Distractions."

"Yeah, I've been distracted, too." His final step left him standing just a foot from her.

Already she longed for his touch. As if he knew that, he reached up to run his fingertip down her cheek. "This is probably not a good idea," she said shakily.

"Probably not. But we ought to make sure. One kiss can't hurt."

Oh, but it could.

And oh, she wished she had the strength to say so.

But Michael dipped his head and her eyes closed automatically and his mouth brushed hers. And suddenly, against her better judgment, she was kissing him back. He slipped his arm around her the way he had at the skating rink. She rested her hand on his broad chest, sure she could feel his heart pounding beneath his T-shirt. His kiss deepened and her head swam, and to her dismay the murmur of satisfaction she gave turned into a little mewling sound…

Or had it?

She stiffened in Michael's arms, recognizing the whimpering sound as Penny's now-familiar announcement of her colic.

Maybe this time it was Penny's way of warning her to stay away from Michael.

Maybe her baby knew best.

Her hand was still resting on his chest. His arm still curved around her waist. She pushed against him and, immediately, he released her. "I need to go to Penny." Darting around him, she fled to the playpen. She scooped her now wailing daughter into her arms and settled her against her chest. Luckily, except for that one time downstairs, she and the baby had been in the housekeeper's room whenever Penny's colic hit.

Looks like that luck had run out.

"How long will she go on like this?" Michael asked, his voice raised above Penny's sharp cries.

His expression was blank, his tone even, and she tried not to read a reproach into his words. "It could be an hour, maybe longer."

He nodded and walked away.

Eyes stinging, she turned her back on him, too.

"*Shh-shh*," she murmured to Penny, pressing a kiss against her soft hair.

This time, when she began pacing the floor, she knew the tactic wouldn't do a thing to help distract her thoughts from Michael. She only hoped she could do a better job of soothing Penny.

Amber walked the floor, rocking Penny against her for what felt like agonizing hours. In real time, she knew only a few minutes had passed. Sadly, she had learned to gauge the length of her daughter's bouts by the rising and eventual tapering off of her cries. Thankfully, those bouts had gotten shorter and shorter.

Yet it had only taken the first few cries to send Michael running from the room.

Obviously, he wanted nothing to do with crying babies. But hadn't she known that already?

So much for her plan to get him to fall in love with Snowflake Valley and her family…and with her and Penny. All right, he'd made it plain he didn't want marriage or kids in his future. But for his sake, she wished that he at least could have parents and brothers and sisters like hers. A family who would give him all the love and support he could ever want.

With a sigh, she continued her pacing, turned, and came to a dead halt.

Earlier, with her back turned to Michael and with Penny crying in her ear, she hadn't heard his retreating footsteps. She assumed he had gone upstairs. She hadn't heard him return, either, but he was approaching from the kitchen carrying a tray with a mug and a plate of cookies.

"What's this?" she asked.

"You never got your tea."

"Tea?"

"When I came out of the office, you said you were headed to the kitchen to make some tea." His grin told her he'd seen right through that story the minute he'd heard it.

Blushing furiously, she ducked her head, resting her cheek against Penny's hair. The baby quieted for a moment, hiccoughed, and then began to cry again.

Michael set the tray on the coffee table. “Here, let me take her.”

She froze.

“Come on, I’m not the Abominable Snowman, or whatever passes for the boogeyman around here. Give me the baby. Relax and have your tea before it gets cold.”

After another hesitation, she put Penny into Michael’s arms. Seeing her daughter cradled in his big hands made Amber’s throat grow tight. Seeing Penny cuddled against his broad, inviting chest made her want to cuddle up with them, too.

He caught her looking at him and smiled. “It’s okay, Mom. I’m not going anywhere. Have a seat.”

She did, mostly because that smile made her knees weak. A wave of warmth rushed through her, one that had nothing to do with the crackling fire just a few feet away.

She watched him pace, holding Penny in place with one hand and supporting her head with the other. “You really do know something about babies, don’t you?” she asked over Penny’s cries. To his credit, he barely winced at the sound of the piercing shrieks.

He nodded.

She settled back on the couch and took a steadying sip of tea.

Considering how comfortably he held Penny, he must have had experience with infants or at least very young babies. Last night, when she had tried to find out more about his family, he’d changed the subject. She was determined to try again. “You told me your stepmom already had kids when she married your dad.”

“Yeah, a few.” He answered grudgingly. After a while, he added, “Carmen had—has—three sons, all with different fathers. All younger than me, and each one more trouble than the next.”

She cringed, wondering where Derek fell in that order. Now she felt doubly glad she had never mentioned his phone call to Michael.

After a while, he said, "Two of them were still in diapers when she married my dad. Then, they had a couple of kids together, almost one right after the other. More boys. We had babies on hand in my house for years."

No wonder he hadn't been happy on Christmas Eve the first time he had heard Penny cry. No wonder he seemed to be…certainly not ecstatic now but taking it in stride. "So you were the oldest. And you wound up caring for them sometimes?"

"Most of the time, after Mama was gone. But you know, we all survived to tell the tales." His laugh didn't hold a bit of humor. "I'm not saying Carmen abandoned us. She was there…somewhere. Usually in her room watching soap operas while the kids settled down—more or less—with the afternoon cartoons in the living room."

Penny had quieted against his chest, as if the sound of his voice soothed her. Or as if she were as interested as her mommy was in hearing his story. Amber took another sip of tea, then held her breath, waiting.

He paced across to the dining area and back again. "Having all that responsibility when I was so young probably has a lot to do with how I feel about family."

He said nothing else, just continued to walk with Penny. The baby's cries had eased more quickly than they ever had. Now, she'd settled down to an occasional whimper and flailing fist as she fought the last of the colic.

Fire crackled. The combined warmth from the flames, the mug in Amber's hands, and the tea she had sipped made her eyelids drift downward. She blinked, forcing her eyes open.

There was nothing she could do about her drifting

thoughts.

Did offering to hold her daughter mean Michael was getting comfortable around Penny? That his views about kids were shifting the slightest bit? That if she just held onto hope, one day he'd want to be a husband and daddy? And to have a family with her?

Her heart raced at the thought of all those possibilities.

She started as the mug slipped from her hands. Her eyelids flew open. When had she closed them again? Had she dreamed that Michael had taken charge of Penny?

But, no, she hadn't dreamed it at all. And she hadn't dropped the mug. Holding the baby in one arm, he had taken the mug from her and was setting it on the tray beside the cookies.

"Oh. Sorry. Guess I zoned out just for a minute."

"Why don't you go ahead and curl up for a while." With his free hand, he took the afghan from the back of the couch, shook it out, and draped it over her. "Penny and I will be fine: Shc's almost asleep, too."

"I should take her—"

"You should sleep while you can. Some extra rest won't hurt either of you."

He moved to the chair beside the couch and sat with Penny lying against his chest. She had uncurled her legs, proof the colic had passed. She would sleep easy now.

And as Amber curled up beneath the afghan and her eyes drifted closed again, she knew she would sleep well, too, trusting Michael with the baby and feeling warm and secure and...loved.

Chapter Fourteen

The next morning, Michael entered the kitchen feeling happier than he had in a long time.

Amber had been asleep on her feet last night. She should probably still be in bed, but instead, humming, she moved around the kitchen. The tune was a Christmas carol, of course. But seeing she was happy, too, he wouldn't complain about it.

Or about the smile she sent his way.

"We still have a lot to do to set up for the auction at noon." She gestured toward the stove, where meat waited in a frying pan set next to a square griddle. "I figure we should be fortified for the morning, and lunch might be later than usual. So we've got pancakes and sausage on the menu today. Is that okay with you?"

"That's great with me. *Kris Kringle Kakes*, I presume?"

She laughed. "Of course not. The Barnetts don't follow in Anatole's footsteps when it comes to naming food."

"Good thing. I couldn't handle that this early." But he was teasing. This morning, seeing her bright smile and hearing her carefree laugh, he could handle anything—even another go-around with Penny and her colic. Not that that had been so bad last night. Penny had seemed to quiet quickly once he'd walked the floor with her.

He stopped by the playpen to check on the sleeping baby. "Looks like an angel now, doesn't she?"

"A Christmas angel?" she teased.

"Don't start. But talking about coming up with names, how did you decide on the baby's?"

Her smile dimmed. She ran her fingertips along the top edge of the playpen. Looking down at her daughter, she said softly, "She's my lucky Penny."

Just as quietly, he said, "What happened, Amber?"

He didn't need to explain. Her one quick breath told him she knew what he was asking. He didn't want to destroy her happy mood, but he wanted—needed—to know why his question about the baby had taken her smile away.

She sighed, not looking at him, and he thought she wouldn't answer. After a while, she said, "I've never been shy about wanting a lot of kids. When I got married, we both agreed we would start a family. And when I got pregnant almost right away, I was overjoyed. But as soon as I told him, he was so *over* it while I was still getting used to the *joy*."

He covered her hand with his.

"We'd been having problems, but I never knew they were that bad." She was silent for a while, then went on, her voice suddenly shaking. "Later the same day I'd told him about the baby, I came home from the grocery store to an empty apartment. I didn't catch on until I saw his phone charger gone from the kitchen counter. Then his razor and toothbrush missing from the bathroom. Drawers in the dresser empty. His half of the closet cleaned out, down to and including the hangers."

And judging by her bleak expression, the discoveries had

ripped out a piece of her heart.

He squeezed her fingers gently. "I'm sorry."

It couldn't help. Nothing he could say would take away the pain she'd lived with for so long. The husband sounded like a louse who had kicked back and enjoyed his perks but didn't want the responsibility that went with them. The friend who borrowed money without paying it back had preyed on her generosity and good nature. And he…

He was no better than they were.

He'd gotten close to her even when they weren't in public.

He had tried to grab what he wanted, without listening to what she'd told him, time and time again. Without facing the truth.

The doorbell rang, startling him. Probably some of her family, since he didn't know anyone else in Snowflake Valley that well. Oddly enough, the thought didn't bother him. Even more odd, he found himself looking forward to seeing any of the Barnetts again.

"I'll get it," Amber said, backing a step away from him. She met his gaze for a moment, then turned and hurried from the room.

After he'd watched her go, he took a seat and stared at the flowers in the Santa sleigh in the middle of the table.

He might not have realized what he'd done to Amber until now, but he'd told her the truth about himself last night. He was used to taking care of babies.

He had been comfortable holding Penny and unexpectedly pleased at knowing he had helped calm her down and get her to sleep. At knowing Amber had felt comfortable enough to drift off and trust him with her baby. He could…

He could care for both Amber and her child. But he'd watched his stepmother undercut everything his dad had tried to do for her kids. How would Amber act in the same situation?

He'd never know. Attempting a permanent relationship, having a family, and especially taking on the role of stepfather weren't choices he was willing to make. He couldn't.

The sound of male voices, then heavy footsteps approaching from the front entry, made him frown. The voices didn't sound like Nick or either of Amber's brothers. But who else would have dropped in this early in the morning at a secluded mountain lodge?

As Amber walked into the kitchen, he found his answer.

She was followed closely by three of the reasons he'd come to the lodge to be alone.

• • •

As she prepared breakfast, Amber discovered the least of her worries was whether or not there were enough sausages to go around.

When the three males standing on the front porch had introduced themselves as Michael's brothers, she had been thrilled. At last, he would have the chance to spend a holiday with his family, to strengthen his bonds with them, as she had hoped.

Then she had walked into the kitchen with Michael's brothers following her. The brief flash of emotion she had caught in his eyes made her hopes evaporate like the water drops she'd used to test the heat of the griddle.

She transferred the last stack of pancakes onto one of the waiting platters and turned toward the table.

"I'm so glad you're here," she said, forcing a bright tone. "And there's no worry at all about putting you up. All the rooms are ready for guests." She glanced at Michael, waiting for him to second her welcome. Foolish hope. Yet, when the other three males turned to look at him, she raised her brows, sending him silent encouragement. Or maybe a plea.

To her relief, he nodded. "Yeah. Glad you could visit."

"Right in time for Snowflake Valley's Winter Festival, too," she said. "Plus, there's an auction opening today." She set the platters of pancakes and sausages on the table and took her seat.

"Right," Michael said. "Your arrival is...good timing."

Derek, the one she had spoken to on the phone, speared a sausage with his fork and took a bite. "That's the way you get ahead in life, taking advantage of things whenever you can."

"One way," Michael said with the faintest edge in his tone.

"So," she said quickly, "where do you all fall in the family order?"

"I'm the fourth," Derek announced. "I've got a different dad than these three guys. And I'm not related to Mike at all. Am I, Mike?"

"Only by marriage," he answered.

Again, she heard that edge in his voice. She pushed away both guilt and relief. Not telling him about her phone conversation with Derek had been the right decision, after all.

She looked at the two boys seated across from her, who had introduced themselves as Raymond and Lee. They appeared to be in their late teens. "And how about you two in the family order?"

"We're half-brothers with Michael," Raymond said. "I'm after Derek and our two older stepbrothers."

No wonder they hadn't built relationships, if they all focused on the divisions in their family instead of possible connections.

Raymond tilted his head toward Lee. "This one's the baby."

"I'll give you baby. I can outwrestle you any day."

"Yeah, right."

Recalling what Michael had told her the other day about flying fists and broken glasses at his family's table, she jumped in. "Well, it's great to meet you all. I'll have to introduce you to my brothers and sisters later."

"Are the girls as hot-looking as you?" Derek asked.

"Derek," Michael said.

The other man shrugged. "Just calling it as I see it."

"Just don't. Amber's your hostess."

"I thought she was the housekeeper."

She wanted to cry at yet another reminder of that fact. She wanted to get out of this situation before Michael found out she had gotten *him* into it. "I *am* the housekeeper. And right now, the cook."

"A great cook," Lee said with a grin that reminded her faintly of Michael's. "The pancakes were awesome."

"Thank you." She smiled back at him.

Like the smell of breakfast sausage, a silence hung over the kitchen. It was broken only by the sounds of forks hitting plates and coffee mugs thumping against the tabletop. So different from mealtimes with her family, when two and three conversations went on at once.

Finally, she said, "I'm glad you arrived in time for breakfast. Michael and I will be leaving soon to help set up for the auction. You're welcome to come, too, and give us a hand. Or just hang out at the festival. Or visit some of the sights in town. There's plenty to see in Snowflake Valley. Isn't there, Michael?"

"Oh, yeah," he said. "You won't want to miss a stop at the Candy Cane."

Now his tone was edged with sarcasm. He was still mocking her hometown. And why did either of those things surprise her? They'd shared a few moments of closeness last night and again this morning. But when it came to their basic differences, nothing had changed.

She blinked to clear her suddenly blurry eyes and turned back to his brothers. She was only the housekeeper and cook, and she was going to act like it. "If you've brought bags with you and would like to get them from your car, I'll take you upstairs to your rooms."

The brothers showed their enthusiasm for her offer by the screech of chair legs on the floor and the stomp of boots across the kitchen. She reached for the empty dishes and rose from her seat.

Michael rested his hand on her arm. The warmth of his fingers nearly made her fumble one of the platters. His dark-eyed gaze, steady on her, made her feel even warmer.

"I apologize for Derek," he said, "since he doesn't have the manners to excuse himself."

"What's to excuse?" she asked flippantly. "What girl wouldn't like being told she's hot-looking?"

"Then *I'll* tell you. You're hot. You're beautiful. And you're—" He snapped his mouth shut and took his hand from her arm.

Her pulse thrummed. *You're...*what*? Off-limits? Taken? Mine?*

"—you're too good for him," he finished.

Heartbroken, she forced herself to say evenly, "I don't know about that. Lately, it seems I'm not good enough for anybody."

"It's not you at all, Amber. It's—" He shook his head. "Forget it. Just don't let my brothers get to you. And don't fall for anything they tell you."

"Then Derek doesn't really think I'm hot-looking?"

He glared at her. "That's not what I mean. Listen, the two younger boys aren't as bad but Derek and his brothers are nothing but trouble."

"Maybe that's because you haven't established a good

relationship with them. But if you tried—"

"I'm done trying."

"But...they're here. You're not going to tell them to leave, are you?"

"No, I won't do that. Especially with another storm front on the way. But don't expect me to be as happy as you seem to feel to have them here. I told you once before, we're a family of mutts. We never spent enough time together to develop relationships. And that's fine by me. In case you haven't picked up on it from what else I've said, I more or less raised myself—and the kids, too, in their earlier years."

At the slamming of the front door and the sound of footsteps, he lowered his voice and spoke in a rush. "Relationships? Family? Forget it. They're nothing but trouble. I've told you how I feel about them."

"Yes, you have," she said sadly, turning away with the empty platters.

Chapter Fifteen

Michael turned off the main street and parked the SUV in the elementary school's lot. They had spent more time than he had expected on the road this morning.

After breakfast, he'd become the chauffer while Amber had acted as hostess and tour guide to his brothers. It was as if the Amber he knew was gone, as if the jacket she wore that turned her eyes so blue had become a uniform. She had given the guys an idea of the town's layout, shown them the most popular tourist attractions, and pointed out the stores and restaurants on Icicle Lane.

As he climbed out of the SUV, he silently acknowledged she had given him an education, too. Despite her businesslike manner, with every word she'd spoken, he had heard the pride in her voice and seen it in her expressions. She loved this town.

He wished he had something in his life he loved even half as much. He wished she—

"Last man to the top of the heap wins," Derek said suddenly, shoving past him and heading toward a pile of snow that had been plowed into one corner of the parking lot.

The other boys, always up to a challenge, hurried after Derek.

Amber was taking a twine-wrapped box out of the back of the SUV. When they had dropped Penny off at Amber's parents' house, Mrs. Barnett had given her a box of homemade sweet rolls to take to the school with them. The scent of cinnamon had filled the vehicle. So had the sound of Derek's voice as he talked nonstop trying to impress Amber.

Michael had clamped his jaws tight to keep his mouth shut.

Too bad he hadn't done that in the kitchen with Amber earlier.

She rounded the front end of the SUV. In the sunlight, her eyes sparkled and her hair shone.

She *was* hot. She *was* beautiful. He hadn't lied.

But he'd been a real jerk during the rest of the conversation.

He ran his hand through his hair. "Amber, this morning I shouldn't have let loose with some of the things I said to you. Or at least, I should have found a better way to say them."

"But you still should have said them, is that what you mean?"

He shrugged. "Yeah. The general message stands. I'm not cut out for having a family. And now you've seen part of the reason for that yourself."

They both stood watching his brothers. Across the lot, Derek had made a snowball. Now, he lobbed it toward Raymond, who ducked. The snowball struck one of the school windows with a jarring *thunk*.

"Hey, watch it!" Michael yelled. "Or are you planning to pay for your own damages this time around?"

"Got you for that, bro," Derek called back, laughing.

Raymond and Lee jumped down from the mound of

snow and headed toward the SUV.

"They're just boys," Amber murmured.

"They're men," he said harshly. "At least Derek's supposed to be. The other two are younger. I'll give them some slack. But even they don't act the way they should, thanks to Derek and his brothers. You don't see Josh and Drew pulling stunts like that, do you? They have more sense."

"Maybe if you'd all spent more time together as they got older, Derek and the rest of them might have turned out differently."

"You're saying I'm at fault."

"Not even close. I know you've been living away from home for a while now. I'm just saying it's too bad that while you were there you didn't have the chance to get closer. But I'm sure you've had more of a good influence on them than you think. I know you would have tried." She paused, then added, "What was that about Derek paying for damages?"

"Something else I shouldn't have said."

She hesitated, as if she planned to push the issue. But Raymond and Lee ran up to them, and she turned to smile at his brothers.

He wished she had sent that smile in his direction first.

• • •

By late morning, they finished transferring all the donated items to the community center.

As much as she could, Amber had kept her eye on Michael's brothers. Easy enough with Derek. He never left the room, just wandered around checking out the prizes. Raymond and Lee helped her brothers and some of the teachers carry boxes into the center.

With Michael, she had tried to do just the opposite—*not* pay attention to what he was doing. At that job, she failed. He and another group of teachers set up tables in the large main room. Watching him work all those muscles of his was a sight too good to miss.

Seeing him headed her way wasn't bad, either. Quickly, she turned to the job that was *supposed* to hold her attention, hanging a display of snowflakes on a tabletop-sized Christmas tree. And she did love the snowflakes. Each one was prettier than the one before.

Michael stopped beside her. "Think anybody's going to bid on these? They're too much of a good thing, aren't they? The tourists have an entire town filled with ornaments for sale."

"People who live here normally *outbid* the tourists for these. They're special. You remember Mrs. Anderson?"

"Of course. I never forget any woman who calls me handsome—"

"Oh, *please*."

"—or who thinks I'll make a great Snow Ball King."

"Well…she might've gotten that part right. Anyway, Mrs. Anderson made these ornaments. She's ninety-seven and the valley's oldest resident. And she's made snowflakes for the festival since she was six years old."

He whistled. "Now, that's a tradition."

"It sure is. She crochets them and sprinkles them with glitter, then adds enough spray starch to make sure the glitter never falls off. When I was little, I always thought the sparkles were the elf equivalent of magic dust."

"I'm betting you still think that." He traced the edge of a snowflake with his fingertip, in the same gentle way he'd touched her face. "Christmas is over, and you're still managing to get your fill of it, aren't you?" She listened but couldn't find any hint of judgment in his tone.

"I'll never get my fill," she said truthfully.

A few feet from them, Callie turned, surveying the room.

"Not bad," she said with satisfaction. "We should bring in quite a bit of money for the school."

"Looks like you made a real killing," Derek said. "You oughta hire me to keep the loot safe while everybody's out having fun."

Amber smiled. It sounded like he was trying to make up for the clowning around he had done this morning. She hoped Michael would take note.

Callie smiled, too. "Thanks for the offer, but we'll lock up as we leave. I think we'll be okay." She turned to the crowd. "All right, gang, according to my watch, it's almost lunchtime. I think you all deserve some time off. But first, can you two give me a hand?" She gestured toward the empty boxes piled in one corner of the room.

She had asked Josh and Drew, but Amber noticed Raymond and Lee followed.

Michael watched them for a moment before turning back to her. The smile he gave her lit his dark eyes, his face…and a special place in her heart.

That smile also left the rest of her heart aching.

Everything he had told her about his past proved he had given up on the idea of a happy future. She understood that. Not so long ago, she had felt the same. But only for a very brief time, because she'd had a baby on the way. A baby she had already loved. She'd had a family she loved and who loved her, too.

He seemed so alone.

If only she could go back to being a little girl who believed in magic elf dust. If only she had some of that special dust now.

Somehow, she had to make Michael believe in the magic of Snowflake Valley.

And before his visit here ended, she needed to make him believe in family.

• • •

For the second time in two days, Michael sat on a bench at the rink.

After a skating pageant put on by the school district, the town had held open competitions. Amber dared him to enter the speed-skating event. He'd signed up for it and walked away with a "silver medal."

The foil-covered cardboard medallion dangled from a red ribbon hung around his neck. It entitled the bearer to two desserts at the Candy Cane. He knew who would share those with him.

He sat listening to Amber charm his brothers. Well, the two youngest ones. Halfway through the pageant, Derek had wandered off on his own somewhere.

"You've never eaten roasted chestnuts?" she asked in exaggerated amazement.

"Go easy on them," Josh said. "These city boys can't help it they've been deprived."

"I'll give you deprived," Raymond said.

Michael tensed.

"And I'll give you guys half my chestnuts," Drew told Raymond. "But only if you'll take that chip off your shoulder."

"What chip?" Raymond demanded, but he grinned as he said it. He yanked Drew's ski cap off his head, then held it out to him. "Fill 'er up."

"Very funny." Laughing, Drew replaced his cap. "Let's go."

The boys headed toward the row of concession stands. Near the stands, the chestnut vendor stood with his wheeled cart.

Finished changing into his boots, Michael took Amber's hand. They followed the boys. The air around the cart was hazy from the heat and smelled like the roasted nuts.

"Have you been deprived, too?" she asked as they joined the line behind their brothers.

"No," he said. "I've eaten plenty of roasted chestnuts."

"Then you know how good they are. I'll share mine with you."

"I'll pass, thanks. You might not want to spoil your appetite, either."

"What do you mean?"

He transferred the medallion from his neck to hers. "I'm officially inviting you to share my dessert. After all, if not for you, I wouldn't have entered the race. You dared me. And you knew I couldn't pass that up." Her flushed cheeks told him she also knew exactly what he meant—though a reminder wouldn't hurt. So he kissed her…just the way he had after their snowball fight.

"Your lips are cold." He wrapped his arms around her and brushed her mouth with his, planning only to torment her for a moment. But her tongue met his in an all-too-teasing touch that shook him from head to toe and stunned a few vital places in between. Talk about torment. He pressed his mouth against hers again, and darned if even the quick kiss she allowed him this time wasn't just as earthshattering. He eased back to meet her gaze. "Now that's more like it. You're getting warmed up. Why don't we see—"

"Michael…"

"That's me," he said, keeping his voice low, "the man with the right to kiss you. We're out in a crowd now, aren't we?" But that didn't matter. They could have been alone, and still, he'd have wanted exactly what he'd just gotten—and more.

"You won that contest on your own," she said.

No surprise she'd gone back to the issue at hand. And definitely no surprise at what she'd said. It always made her uncomfortable to take credit for anything. He thought again about how often she praised her family…something he'd never felt a reason to do with his.

As if she'd read his thought, she said, "You should share the wealth with your brothers."

"Believe me, I do." He regretted his irritated tone as soon as the words left his mouth. Amber frowned, and he had only himself to blame. Too late to take the words back. But, he hoped, not too late to keep from spoiling their afternoon. He looked down at the medallion lying against her jacket, then back at her. "I want to share this with *you.*"

She ran her finger along the ribbon. "Thanks. In that case we should step out of line. I'll pass on the chestnuts, too."

They moved over to wait by the wooden building. As she leaned back against the outer wall, he moved to stand in front of her. His body cast a shadow over her face but did nothing to dim the light in her eyes.

"I need to save my appetite for Anatole's desserts," she said. "Besides, we still have hot dogs and toasted marshmallows ahead of us at the Christmas campfire tonight."

"Really? I could get used to this."

"It would be easy to do," she whispered, her voice soft, drawing him to her.

Lots of things would be easy for him to do right now. Run his fingers through her hair. Cup her cheek with his palm. Kiss her lips again. Right now. Right here. He wanted all those things, all at once. He wanted an entire list of things he couldn't have.

He reached for the foil disk and hefted it in his hand, as if it had the weight of a real medallion.

She glanced down. "You look like you're about to toss a coin."

"Maybe I am. Heads, I win. Tails, I win, too. Because when it comes to you, how could anyone lose?"

Her eyes shimmered.

He hesitated, then went on. “What you said this morning–about not being good enough for anyone. That wasn’t true. The guy who left you…you picked the wrong man, that’s all.”

“And the right one?”

As always, from the day he’d met her, he could read her expressions. He could see her emotions in her eyes. Her face was so open. So sincere. So Amber.

Now, he knew what she was asking. And he didn’t have the right answer. But he’d started this and he had to finish it and he had to tell her the truth.

He shook his head. “Not me, sweetheart. No matter how much I’d want to, I could never be the right man for you.”

Chapter Sixteen

Supper at the campfire had gone exactly as Michael had anticipated, with everybody skewering hot dogs and marshmallows over the flames. Then the big, noisy group turned to the traditional sing-along. Only, naturally, Snowflake Valley's entertainment leaned heavily toward Christmas carols.

He liked listening to Amber's sweet voice as she carried the tunes and hit the high notes. And he appreciated that she seemed herself even after he'd been honest with her. At least they'd gotten that out in the open. Out of their way.

The days were moving along faster than he'd skated in the competition. Their pretend dating would end soon. But he'd enjoy that, too, while it lasted. And he had to keep up appearances for Amber.

As the crowd broke up and people began to straggle in different directions, he wrapped his arm around her shoulders. "I'm impressed, same as the night we went caroling. I didn't tell you then, but I should have. You sing like a Christmas angel."

The thought had hit his brain and escaped through his mouth before he could stop it. Ruefully, he shook his head. Even *he* was being infected by the Christmas spirit around here. But he'd meant what he said. She blushed at the compliment, something he'd never get tired of seeing.

Nick and Lyssa walked up to them, their arms around each other.

Michael eased a step away from Amber. Better to be safe. When he was around her, he had less control over his hands than he did over his mouth.

"Guess you've one-upped me in the medal department," Nick said.

He forced a laugh. "Buddy, I've left you so far behind, you'll never catch up."

"Who needs medals?" Lyssa asked, waving her hand as if brushing the idea away. Waving her hand again, as if he hadn't seen it the first time. Waving her hand a third time—and then Amber let out a squeal to rival one of her daughter's.

"You've got your ring!" Her face lit with pleasure and joy.

A feeling he couldn't name thumped inside his chest.

Lyssa held her hand up, ring facing out. "Nick was planning to give it to me at the ball tomorrow night, but I couldn't wait. I love my temporary engagement ring, but I love this one better."

"I know you do," Amber said. She touched the medallion hanging from its ribbon.

Why she'd done that, he couldn't tell. Maybe he didn't want to know. But the action reminded him of his promise. And gave him something to do besides worry about keeping his hands to himself. "What do you say? Everybody ready for dessert?"

"Sounds good to me," Nick agreed. "Those marshmallows over the campfire only whet my appetite for something sweet."

The way Amber whets mine.

She was his something sweet.

Too sweet. Too hurt. Too surrounded by family.

"Let's go, then," Lyssa said. "There will be a waiting line at the Candy Cane."

Amber had told him the businesses on Icicle Lane stayed open later than usual this time of year, taking advantage of the additional tourists here for the festival. Night had fallen a long while ago, but the area was as bright as day. Strings of colored lights arced across the street between the posts. Wavy rectangles of light shining through store windows and doorways made the sidewalks look like rivers of gold.

He shook his head.

Amber glanced up. "What's wrong?" she asked quietly under the noise of the conversations around them.

"Nothing. I was just thinking everything seems..." He laughed sheepishly, then finished, "...magical, I guess. Must be why you like it so much."

He heard her sharp intake of breath. As if to cover the reaction, she opened her eyes and mouth wide in exaggerated surprise. "Oh, my. Is that really *you* talking, Scrooge? Can it be you're beginning to mellow?"

"I didn't say *I* liked the place," he protested, laughing again.

"Ah...but that's the thing about Snowflake Valley. It's not just a place, it's a feeling. You're beginning to see why the town's special, and that's how the feeling starts." Her voice rang with confidence. "Before you know it, you'll be volunteering to play Santa."

"I doubt that."

"Well, later, don't say I didn't tell you so." Smiling, she linked her arm with his.

• • •

Dessert at the Candy Cane was all Amber could have wished for—though she couldn't care less whether or not she ate any of Anatole's sweet creations. She already rode on a sweet, wonderful, emotional high. She held onto hope. She revived her dying dreams.

Wow. Lyssa might be right about her occasional dramatics. And maybe she *was* overreacting. But she couldn't let the realities of life drag her down twenty-four seven. She had to trust in her belief in Snowflake Valley.

After all, Michael had admitted he found her beloved town magical.

And now, he sat beside her with his arm across the back of her chair. Unlike their previous visit to the Candy Cane, his hand most definitely touched her shoulder.

"Hey, Raymond," he said, raising his voice slightly above the noisy crowd, "I know you like coconut. You'll have to try the *Toasted Reindeer Treats*."

Raymond fumbled his unopened menu. "You want me to eat reindeer food?"

"It's just the name they call it. Don't worry, you'll get used to that." Michael looked down at his menu, then at Amber.

She smiled up at him. "Have you gotten used to it?"

"I think so. In fact, I'm looking forward to my *Alpine Angel Cake*."

You sing like a Christmas angel.

She didn't, of course, but the memory of his compliment gave her the same shiver of pleasure now that it had brought on then.

She relayed her order to their overworked waitress, who nodded and smiled. All the employees here were used to being busy during festival week.

As the others gave their orders, Amber glanced around the room. Again, they had taken the largest table, although they'd added a few more chairs tonight. All three of Michael's brothers had joined them. And on their way to the Candy Cane, Lyssa had phoned Mom and Dad, who had arrived with Penny.

This made the seating even tighter than last time. She didn't mind, not when she could catch a faint scent of Michael's aftershave and feel the heat of his body so close to hers.

She flushed, then swallowed a laugh at her reaction to her own thought. It wasn't as if anyone could read her mind. Still, knowing her cheeks had to be flaming, she leaned over to check on Penny, who lay in her carrier on the chair beside hers. The baby slept quietly.

Amber looked down the length of the table.

Derek had caught up with their group as they reached the Candy Cane. He sat at the foot of the table, his focus wandering around the room. The other four boys all seemed to get along well. Michael's two youngest brother weren't shy about talking to the twins, either.

She hoped the girls would never join the ranks of the "bad-luck Barnett sisters," the way she and Callie and Lyssa had. Now, Lyssa had given up the title. Amber hoped she wouldn't have to carry it forever, either. She touched the medallion resting against her sweater.

Michael must have noticed. "That's not as good as the real thing."

"It could be. It's all in how you look at it."

"Well, that's true. Most of them don't come with a free dessert attached."

That hadn't been what she'd meant. Receiving the medal as a gift from Michael made it special to her. In the same way, Lyssa's temporary ring would always hold a place in her heart—and in the Barnett family's memories and photo albums...

The albums that held the kind of group pictures Michael

had mocked.

A small twinge of doubt ran through her. But if he had changed his mind about the magic of Snowflake Valley, he could change his mind about family photos...and about a family of his own.

Couldn't he?

Forget doubts. She needed positive thinking here. With the effort that took, she barely tasted her dessert. She missed most of the conversation. She only noticed Derek standing to leave because he shoved his chair back so abruptly. The sound of the legs screeching against the wooden floor drowned out the chatter in the room.

Penny let out a startled cry. Amber patted her daughter's arm.

Everyone looked at Derek.

"I'll meet you guys at the truck." He gestured at the mugs and plates on the table. "You got this, right, Mike?"

"Sure," Michael said.

He spoke easily. Though she listened for it, she didn't hear a false note in his tone. But a second later she saw, half-hidden by the tablecloth, his fingers curl into a fist on his thigh.

• • •

Home at the lodge, Michael went alone to his office. It took a while, but finally, he felt much better than he had with Derek at the Candy Cane. He powered down his computer and sat back in the desk chair, reviewing the situation.

It was bad enough the man had never picked up a check in his life. He didn't need to call attention to his freeloading habit in front of all the Barnetts.

When he had walked off, Mr. Barnett and Nick tossed some bills onto the table. Michael appreciated that. Not because he wouldn't willingly have paid the entire tab again, but because the other men had stepped up to ease the awkward moment. It said a lot that he had friends who had done what family—what Derek—had refused to do.

On the slow walk through town to where he'd parked the SUV, the frigid air had cooled some of his anger. The good-natured teasing he'd gotten from all four of the younger boys had taken care of the rest. They'd threatened to challenge him to a skating rematch.

Let them try and beat his record. He didn't care. They'd just better not plan to get their hands on his medal. Amber's medal now.

He smiled. She'd sure seemed attached to it. Well, that made sense. She loved shiny objects like those glittery handmade snowflakes.

Like Lyssa's bright and shiny engagement ring.

Again, that feeling he'd had at seeing Amber's joy kicked inside his chest. He thought he had figured out what the feeling meant. But he wasn't about to give a name to it.

"Hey, Mike." Derek. Didn't even need to recognize the voice to know. Nobody else called him that.

He looked up, taking in his stepbrother's swagger, his expression, the look in the eyes. All familiar, and all spelling trouble. "What can I do for you?" he asked shortly, anticipating the confidence he would hear in that voice, too.

"Nothing much." Derek grinned. He needed a good shave and some dental work on a tooth he'd had broken in a fistfight. "I could use a loan—just a small one to tide me over." He had made a good call with that last addition. Probably knew small would be his only option. He wasn't dumb by any means. He just didn't have a very good memory.

"What happened to the thousand dollars I gave you? On Christmas Eve, remember? That wasn't even a week ago."

It was the night he'd walked into the lodge and almost

gotten brained by a ceramic elf. Less than a week since he'd first kissed Amber. Only a few days since he'd…

Stop right there. Luckily, Derek's whine distracted him.

"I spent that money. I needed it, man. And now I need more. I've got a deal working."

"Here in Snowflake Valley?"

"Maybe." Derek grinned again.

"You haven't been here long enough to make any connections." Then where had he gone off to this afternoon? His stomach knotted. That would be all he'd need, to find out Derek was up to no good in this town. Indirectly or not, *he* was the one who had brought his stepbrother here. The one who might unintentionally have opened the door to something that would affect Amber. "Stay away from the folks in the valley."

Derek scowled. "You can't tell me who I can and can't be friends with. What do you know, anyhow? And what about that loan?"

"Forget the loan. I'm not carrying extra cash with me."

"What the— Come on, Mike, don't try to play me. They got ATMs in this hick town, don't they?"

"Probably. I'm not going near one tonight. Or tomorrow."

"You're a big help, man."

"Wrong. I *was* a big help. Now it's time for you to help yourself."

Muttering a curse, Derek swung away from the desk. He stomped across to the doorway and disappeared through it.

Michael sat back in his chair. He stared at the tall window off to one side of the room, but all he saw was his reflection bounced back at him from the glass.

That, and a small ceramic Santa sitting on the windowsill, looking at him. Funny, he hadn't seen the ornament before tonight. But he knew exactly how the thing had gotten there. And it didn't involve magic or even Santa Claus himself.

A moment later, he heard footsteps. He turned to find Amber standing just inside the office doorway. "Is everything okay?" she asked. "The boys and I were in the kitchen, and we…we heard some shouting."

"Oh, everything's fine," he said with forced breeziness. "Just another action-packed episode in the life of my happy family."

She crossed to the desk and said in a low voice, "I saw Derek headed upstairs. He didn't look happy. Neither do you."

"I was being sarcastic."

She smiled sadly. "I figured that out." She ran her finger along the edge of the desk. "Michael, I know you didn't have the best time growing up. And I can see why you might feel some…some disappointment in Derek."

"Disappointment?"

"Well…frustration. Anger. Whatever."

"Yeah. All of the above. Especially the whatever."

"I'm sorry." She met his gaze, her blue eyes steady and bright, her chin set stubbornly. "Raymond and Lee seem like good kids. They're fun and friendly, willing to cooperate and help out. Maybe you could spend more time with them. I'm sure they'd like that…" He shrugged. When he said nothing, she added, "You must have *some* good memories of growing up with them."

Any positive thoughts her earlier words might have triggered disappeared in a flash.

"These are my memories," he said flatly. "Taking care of a bunch of kids on my own. Having my dad work so much he never came home. And listening to my stepmother make excuses for bailing her sons out of jail."

Now, what positive spin would she try to put on that news?

He might never know. Lee called to her from the living room and, after another glance at him, she left the office.

Chapter Seventeen

To say breakfast had been awkward was an understatement.

Derek had made no effort to hide his irritation at having his loan denied.

Maybe you could spend more time with them…

At the memory of Amber's words, Michael had a hard time hiding his irritation at Derek, too. But he'd shut up on that subject, both last night and at breakfast. In the long run, seeing his stepbrother's true colors would give Amber a better idea of what he'd meant about his family.

He was almost glad when Derek insisted on driving down to the valley alone.

"I need my wheels, man. You never know when something might come up." He grinned. "Like maybe you'll need me to pick up some stuff for the auction."

"That's nice of you to volunteer," Amber told him. "And I need to take my own car today, too. I have some errands to run, and later, I'll have to drop Penny off at a friend's house. My mom and dad will be as busy as we are this afternoon and at the ball tonight."

"Your whole family's going to be there, right?" Raymond asked.

"Oh, yes," she said with a smile. "None of us would miss it."

Both Raymond and Lee looked happy at hearing her answer.

Michael had been less happy about losing the chance to ride alone with her and Penny. He'd taken the two younger boys along with him. In convoy, they'd headed down the mountain and into Snowflake Valley.

Callie and her teacher friends had taken the first shift at the community center. He and Amber—and the boys—were all free until after lunch.

They agreed to meet at the local arcade. Not too long after he'd arrived with the boys, Amber showed up, with both her brothers along for the ride.

"I should have guessed," he told her. "Even the games here have a holiday theme. Little kids fishing for Christmas ornaments instead of goldfish. Playing 'Submerge the Santa' instead of 'Dunk the Clown.' And nowhere else but in Snowflake Valley would they think of this." He gestured at what should have been the bottle toss. In this town, players tried to settle plastic wreaths around pint-sized pine trees.

"What do you think," Amber asked. "Are you ready to give it a shot?"

"Why not?" He handed over a couple of dollars and received a handful of wreaths. They made him think of the medallion and ribbon he had won yesterday, then given to Amber.

The trees made him think of twinkling lights reflecting in golden-brown hair.

Everything in this town reminded him of Amber and Christmas and family and other things he didn't want to think about. But there was no getting away from any of those things today.

He tossed a wreath and watched it bounce off the star on top of a tree. Luckily, Amber had turned to talk to one of Callie's teacher friends.

A few feet away, Raymond and Lee stood talking with Nick.

"Sorry about him putting you and Mr. Barnett and Michael on the spot last night," Raymond said.

"Yeah, me, too," Lee said. "He's a real jerk sometimes."

They were apologizing to Nick for Derek's behavior, the same way he'd done to Amber after Derek's crack about her. He didn't like seeing the boys' embarrassment. He didn't like knowing they felt the need to take on that responsibility. But he respected them for stepping up.

"No worries," Nick told them. "I may not have brothers or sisters, but I know you've got to take the bad with the good in a family. Or, from what I can tell from the Barnetts, you can just focus on the good."

"Works for me." Raymond walked off with Nick.

Michael turned back to the game.

Lee moved up to stand beside him. He held several of the wreaths. Laughing, he shook his head. "I'm not having much luck with this one."

"It's harder than it looks," Michael agreed. That was true for too many things in life. He thought of something else Amber had said last night. Not about Derek but a compliment regarding his younger brothers. "You and Raymond did some good work yesterday, helping out with setting up for the auction. Thanks."

"No problem." Lee tossed a wreath that went wide, then said, "Hey, Michael..."

"What's up?"

He shrugged. "Just wanted to say thanks to you, too. Raymond and I weren't sure you'd want us coming here, but

Derek said you wouldn't mind putting us up."

Exactly what freeloader Derek would say. He skipped over that fact, as well as mentioning any specific names, and went to the important part. "I'm glad you came."

Lee grinned. "Me, too."

"If you stick around a few days, we can do some skiing."

"We have to leave tomorrow to get back for school. Maybe some other time?" Lee sounded hopeful.

"Yeah, that would be good." He'd forgotten he wouldn't be around that long himself. The thought didn't sit right. Probably because *he'd* be sitting behind a desk again, doing his paper-pushing job. But he'd arrange another ski trip at the lodge, and it wouldn't be too long before he'd be back in Snowflake Valley. That thought didn't bother him at all.

He'd meant his offer to Lee, and he'd been happy to hear the boy's hopeful tone. Didn't mean he'd get all sappy and big brotherly, looking back fondly at the days he had changed Raymond and Lee's diapers on a regular basis. The truth, though…Amber's comments about the boys had made him do some thinking. Some remembering.

He hadn't been kidding when he'd told her about Carmen bailing out her older sons, his stepbrothers. But the two youngest boys, his half-brothers, had always caused less trouble than the rest. Maybe Amber was right, and his job taking care of them as kids *had* made a difference.

Or maybe he'd just let her optimism get to him.

And it wasn't only Amber.

He'd tried to hang onto his belief that families were nothing but trouble. Instead, she and her parents and brothers and sisters had shown him how supportive and loving a family could be. As Nick had said to the boys a few minutes ago, the Barnetts focused on the positive.

He was beginning to believe they had the right idea.

His next wreath clattered to the table and bounced

up against one of the trees. He turned to Lee. "That long weekend you're off from school in February. We'll still have plenty of snow here." *We'll?* He shoved the thought aside. "Plan to come up with me then. I'll put it on my schedule."

"Me, too," Lee said. "I'll go find Raymond and tell him."

"Do that."

Lee walked away. Smiling, Michael tossed his last wreath and watched it settle into place around a star-topped tree. He looked in Amber's direction.

Her conversation had ended. She eyed him, her lips curving gently. "See, it's not so hard, is it?"

"You don't think so? Why don't you give it a try?"

"I'm not talking about tossing a wreath," she said softly. "And you know it."

She had overheard his conversation with Lee. Shrugging, he glanced at the wall display of prizes. "Go ahead and take your pick."

"No, thanks. You've already given me a gift."

"The medal and dessert? That was yesterday. Today's a new day."

"That's not what I meant. Although you're right about it being a new day." She gave him the gift of her brilliant smile.

He smiled back. Then he looked at the wall again and nodded to the man behind the counter. "I'll take the one on the second shelf, far left." The man handed him the small bean-filled doll. Michael held it up to show Amber. "Think Penny will like it?"

"She'll love it. It's a Santa." Her smile grew as broad as the doll's. "I'll keep it for her Christmas collection."

Of course. He thought he'd given her something special for the baby. But naturally a mom like Amber, who lived for the holiday, would have her daughter covered. "I should have known she would already have a Christmas collection."

She blushed. "Well, actually…this will be the first item

in it."

"Good. We've all got to start somewhere." He handed her the Santa, then couldn't resist dropping a kiss on her cheek.

• • •

After lunch, they reported to the community center to work the final hours of the silent auction. Once it had closed, the crew split up, half to check the bids and draw the names of the winners. The other half of the crew began cleaning and rearranging the room for tonight.

Amber helped set aside the prizes in a back room, where they would stay until claimed. The auction had been a huge success. She was thrilled for both Callie and the elementary school.

She was also thrilled for herself. This morning, between Michael's conversation with Lee and the gift he'd won for Penny, he had made so much progress toward accepting *family* and *Christmas.*

He might not know it, but the magic of Snowflake Valley was settling on him like the first snowflakes of the season.

She desperately needed some of that magic, too. The clock was ticking. Soon, Michael would leave town. But she still had some time. And she still had tonight to look forward to…

In only a few hours, she would be at the Snow Ball. When the crowd counted down to midnight, she wanted to be in Michael's arms. That meant more to her than anything. More than the possibility of winning the Snow Ball Queen crown.

I don't know about me, but Amber's a sure win for Queen.

She smiled. Michael had said that at the skating rink. And, growing up, she'd coveted that crown. But now winning one seemed so much less important. For her. And even for Michael.

Since he had agreed to run for Snow Ball King, she'd seen

him in conversation with Mayor Corrigan several times, and at least once with almost every member of the town council. They liked Michael for himself. Whether or not he became King, she felt sure he would get his contract.

Whether or not he won didn't matter to her, either. He'd still be her Prince Charming.

For now, she had the pleasure of watching her prince from across the room. Once in a while, she caught him looking in her direction. Every glance kicked up her anticipation.

On a break, she found him in the community center's kitchen.

"Lemonade?" He handed her the paper cup he was holding, then filled another one for himself. "So, what time's the dance tonight?"

"It starts at eight, but I'll have to be here early. I'll go back up to the lodge before then to get ready and get into my dress."

"A dress?"

"Yes. Why so surprised?"

"Maybe because I've never seen you wear one before. But you can bet that's something I'll be wanting to see tonight."

She smiled up at him. A warm cozy feeling settled inside her at knowing he would be thinking of her. That he might be looking forward to the ball as much as she was.

Raymond and Lee entered the kitchen. As they approached, the sight of their wooden expressions made her smile slip away.

Michael must have noticed their faces, too. "What's going on?"

"We're leaving," Lee said.

He frowned. "I thought you were staying for the dance tonight and heading out in the morning."

"Derek wants to go home now. On the radio, they said the storm front passed, and he wants to get going before another one hits. He's got the truck pulled around to the front of the building."

"I see." Michael dropped the crumpled cup in the trash. "What about your stuff?"

"We loaded everything into the truck after breakfast this morning," Raymond admitted. "He said after he yelled at you last night, you'd kick us out sometime today, anyway."

"That would never happen. You believed him?"

"No," Lee protested. "But he's our ride home."

"You don't need to miss the party. I can arrange flights for you two tomorrow."

"That's okay," Raymond said. "We'd better head back with him, or he'll probably get lost on the way."

"And he..." Lee hesitated, then said in a rush, "He said he doesn't want to talk to you. He didn't want us to tell you we were leaving. But we told him we had to say good-bye to you and Amber and the rest of the Barnetts."

"Good for you." Michael shook hands with them both. "Don't forget we're on for the ski party in February. I'll be in touch to make arrangements."

You won't need to rely on Derek for a ride.

Amber could hear the words Michael had been too kind to say.

As the boys headed across the room toward Lyssa and Nick, she slipped her arm through Michael's. "You should be proud of them for coming back in to say good-bye," she told him quietly. "As proud of them as I am of you."

"Me? For what?"

"For not letting Derek get to you. For complimenting Raymond and Lee. And most of all, for not going back on your promise to them."

"If it hadn't been for you, I might not even have made that promise."

"And I didn't even have to dare you."

His smile made her insides tremble. "No, you didn't." His

kiss left her head swimming. The tang of lemonade mixed with the taste of Michael. Forget lightheaded. She was ready for a good old-fashioned faint, right into his arms. "Are you blaming me for your promise?"

"Does this look like blame? I'm thanking you."

He kissed her again, and she wished she had the nerve to respond the way she had at the skating rink. But she didn't. Not here. Not now, in front of so many friends and family. Not when that response of hers had left her melting like a sun-warmed snowman. Later though… "You can thank me again any time," she said with a laugh.

One of the teachers waved to Michael. "We've got reinforcements on the drinks. Want to give me a hand?"

"Sure."

She watched the men lift a huge metal cooler and set it on the countertop. Mental note. The coolers would have to be refilled for the party tonight. Along with the soft drinks she had mentioned to Michael, they would have sweet tea and lemonade.

Plenty of lemonade. She licked her lip.

Callie entered the kitchen doorway and paused, looking their way. She was smiling, but Amber tensed. Just as with Michael's brothers, she saw the stiffness in that expression. Michael had noticed her noticing now, too.

"I'd better go see what's up," she murmured.

Before she could reach the doorway, Callie turned away, heading across the main room and then down the hall to the community center's back office. Amber followed, trying to walk casually. She passed the room where they had stored the auction prizes, then made her way to the office.

Callie stood beside the desk. Lyssa had taken the seat behind it.

One look at their faces made Amber's heart sink.

• • •

As Michael grabbed another cup of lemonade, one of the teachers stopped to wish him good luck in the competition. Even before the man had turned away, Michael's thoughts flew to Amber and what she'd look like wearing a crown. What that dress of hers would look like. How many times he'd get to dance with her.

She had gone down the hall after that unspoken summons from her sister. Callie had seemed calm enough. But something about her manner reminded him of his brothers when they'd come to deliver their bad news. And Amber had stayed by his side while he received it.

He tossed the empty cup in the trash and headed across the room. He'd made it halfway down the hall when she came out of the office. Her shaken expression made him rest a steadying hand on her shoulder. "What is it?"

She shot a look past him, then motioned toward the storage room. Inside, she closed the door and turned to him, her eyes misty. "We're missing money from the auction."

A fist seemed to slam into his gut. *No wonder Derek was in such a hurry to get away.* "All of it?"

"We haven't taken it all in yet. There are some coins left, and a pile of checks from local people. But the rest of what we collected so far is gone."

"Have you called the police?"

She shook her head. "Not yet. Callie knows making this public would spoil the night and probably the whole festival."

And for Amber it would take away some of the magic of Snowflake Valley.

"I'll make good on the money," he said.

"You don't have to do that."

"It's not a case of have to, it's want to. Thanks to you and your family, I…I've been involved with this auction from the beginning. I'm just as invested in the outcome as you all are." He forced a grin. "And I worked just as hard as everyone else did."

"That doesn't mean you have to take money out of your own pocket."

"Why not? I told you that's where my heart is. In my wallet. Let's just call it a donation."

She blinked, then looked away.

When he got his hands on his thieving, freeloading stepbrother… "It was Derek," he said flatly.

"You can't know that," she said, her voice soft.

"I do know it."

"We can't accuse anyone without proof."

"I'm telling you, it was Derek. He was ticked off because I refused to give him another handout last night. And it's my fault he was here in Snowflake Valley to begin with."

"No, it's mine."

He frowned. "What do you mean?"

"He called the lodge the other day," she said with obvious reluctance. "I told him about the festival."

"You didn't think to mention the call to me?"

"He told me not to."

"And you take orders from him?" He struggled to keep his breathing steady. Just the thought of what she had done, when she knew how he felt… "I'm your boss, remember? The owner of that lodge. And you invited guests to drop in—"

"No, I—"

"—and worse, you set up that unwanted reunion."

"I didn't set it up." Her voice faltered. "But I admit, I had hoped—"

"I know what you hoped, but it didn't happen. And it's never going to happen. As I keep telling you, all families are not like yours." Holding back a sigh, he shoved his hand through his hair. "Your sisters, your brothers, your parents—

they all see me as a person. The way you do. My family sees me as a handy source of income."

"That's not true. Look at Raymond and Lee. They didn't mention coming back to the valley for a ski party. You did. They don't want anything from you, except the chance to be with you. Not everyone's like Derek."

This time, he did sigh. "You don't get it. You can't. You didn't grow up in a family like mine. We can debate this for the rest of our lives. But we can't change it. Or the real problem here. And we both know it." He reached toward her, then let his hand drop. "You believe in things that I don't. Christmas and holidays and magic and family."

"And you," she said softly. "I believe in you. I can't change that, either."

"Don't think about me. Think about yourself. And Penny."

Her family of two. One he couldn't make a family of three, no matter how much he might want to be with her. Not with his history.

Whether she had engineered his family reunion—or would admit to it—didn't matter, either. She had hoped for it, ignoring everything he'd told her. He should've trusted his gut all along.

Amber lived in a fantasy town a world apart from his reality. And considering everything she loved and believed in, getting more involved with her might work for the short-term. For a few weeks, they'd do fine. But the Barnetts would take him in—hadn't they already?—and soon holiday would pile on holiday, then birthday on birthday. The family events would only remind Amber of the kids she wanted to have. Would only drag up old memories he'd spent years trying to outrun.

They'd both be better off if this fake relationship ended now.

But, unable to say those words, he yanked open the door and left the room.

Chapter Eighteen

Somehow, Amber managed to slip away from the community center unnoticed while everyone else was still working.

She felt doubly thankful that she had driven her own car this morning and left Penny at her friend's house until later tonight.

She had raced up the mountainside, intent on the idea of taking a quick shower and leaving again before Michael arrived home—*at the lodge.* Although, there didn't seem any point in attending the ball. Her heart wasn't in it anymore. Not when she would be forced to watch Michael from a distance.

Her eyes blurred, making her blink to focus on the snow-covered road. But she could still see and hear him lashing out at her without giving her the benefit of the doubt. Without allowing her a chance to explain. His reaction shouldn't have come as such a shock. Hadn't he told her all along how he felt about his family?

And maybe, in the long run, he had done her a favor, helping her prove her bad judgment with her ex wasn't just a one-shot deal.

She should have known she couldn't trust herself, even when it came to Michael. Especially when it came to him.

Later, after her shower and with her hair slightly damp yet, she drove down the mountainside. Wanting to avoid any questions from her family, she went straight to the community center again.

Not a good idea. If she hadn't been so upset, she would have realized Callie would be there early, too. Her sister took one look at her and tilted her head, indicating Amber should follow her.

In the back office, Amber took a seat on a visitor's chair, being careful not to crease her dress. Her pretty hunter-green mini-dress covered with spangles that she had hoped would knock Michael into next year. So to speak.

I know what you hoped, but it didn't happen.

No, he hadn't had the happy reunion with his family that she had wished for him.

And it wouldn't matter now *how* she looked when he saw her at the ball.

"You don't answer your cell phone anymore?" Callie asked.

"The reception's been awful."

"So has communication around here. Why did you run out on us this afternoon?"

She smoothed the hem of her dress. "I wanted some time to think. I...I talked to Michael just before I left. About the missing money. He thinks Derek took it."

"He might have."

Amber's head snapped up. "What do you mean?"

"Derek's a perfect clone of some of the students I've taught—cocky and overconfident and sure they'll never get caught cheating. Or stealing. And that's just what *this* sounds like. I found it mixed in with the checks we'd gotten for the auction bids." She handed over a small rectangle of paper.

Amber swallowed hard.

On the paper in block letters was written: I HELPED MYSELF.

Last night, she had stood frozen in the doorway near the dining area, unable to miss hearing the raised voices from Michael's office. Seconds later, Derek had stormed out of that room…just after Michael had said *Now it's time for you to help yourself.*

She had been so self-righteous this afternoon, explaining to him about his own family as if she knew them better than he did. But he had been right about Derek.

He had already felt guilty, though it had been her fault Derek had come to Snowflake Valley, not his. And now he would feel even worse, even more responsible.

"I'll tell Michael," she said, already dreading the conversation.

Callie nodded. "And I'll report the theft."

"Do you have to? Can't we keep this from getting out to everyone?" She owed Michael that. He had hurt her…but at least he hadn't done it publicly. And at least her family wouldn't be the ones tying his name to the theft. "Please don't report it, Callie. Michael already told me he'll make up the loss. He's going to give us a donation to cover the missing money."

"He is?" Callie paused, then said thoughtfully, "I don't like the idea of word getting out any more than you do. And if Michael steps in, we're not short any of the money." She nodded decisively. "Okay. I'll run it by everybody at home. It's nice of him to be willing to do that. Very nice." She smiled. "Good men like that don't come along too often, Amber. Don't let him get away."

• • •

Michael adjusted his shirt cuffs and glanced around the crowded community center. He'd been here for a half-hour already and hadn't seen a sign of Amber. Not that he was looking for her.

Nick walked up to him.

"Where's Amber?" he blurted. "Ah...and Lyssa and Callie?"

"I'll bet I can guess which of those three you really want to find. But to answer your questions, all the women are in the back office."

Discussing his offer to pay back the stolen money. He hoped. As he'd told Amber in the heat of the moment, it wasn't the *have to* but the *want to* that drove him to make the offer.

He froze.

That simple sentence made him see so much. He *wanted* to replace the money. Not to protect Derek or even to save face himself. But because he felt he owed it to Snowflake Valley. And to Amber, her baby, and her family. Somehow, in just these few days, he'd gotten attached to them all.

An attachment he'd severed this afternoon, at least as far as Amber was concerned.

Nick nudged him with his elbow. "There you go, buddy. Your wish is granted."

Amber stood in the doorway leading from the hall.

With one glance, his mouth dried and his throat tightened, and swallowing hard nearly left him choking. In this room decorated to the hilt with streamers and spangles and glittering New Year's hats and noisemakers, she was the brightest, most beautiful sight in view. The green dress she wore was just snug enough, just short enough, just sparkly enough to make his imagination—and a few body parts—race to attention.

The sounds of cymbals crashing made him jump. The

band's drummer was calling everyone to order. He managed to drag his gaze away from Amber.

On the stage at the front of the room, Mayor Corrigan stood at the podium. "Well, I know you're not here just to listen to me," he said with a laugh. "We're all ready to have fun tonight, so let's get to the first and very special part of the evening. I have in this envelope the names of Snowflake Valley's new Snow Ball King and Queen and their attendants."

Michael shoved his hands into his pockets so no one would see him crossing his fingers. Not for himself, for Amber. He didn't give a darn about wearing a crown. But she did.

The mayor ran through a few names, calling the runners-up to the front of the room.

He was surprised to note he'd met every one of those men and women this week.

The crowd suddenly hushed, which had to mean the mayor was about to announce the final names. Now, his throat felt so tight, he didn't have the power to swallow.

As the mayor called the next name, the roar of the crowd nearly took the roof off the place.

With ringing ears and blurry eyes, he watched Amber walk to the front of the room to be congratulated. She bowed her head to accept her crown.

The jewels in the crown glittered. Her dress sparkled. Her face glowed. She looked as if she'd been born to be Queen.

Nick slapped him on the back. "Congrats, buddy." At Michael's questioning look, he laughed. "Boy, do you have it bad. Didn't you hear the mayor call your name?"

He glanced at Amber, who stood tall and proud. She sent him a model-worthy smile. And her blue eyes seemed to look right through him.

Once he'd gone to stand beside her and receive his crown, the mayor announced the King and Queen would kick off the dancing for the evening. Michael bowed to Amber and held out his hand. When she hesitated, his heart dropped to the polished toes of his shoes.

Then she smiled, took his hand, and let him sweep her into his arms.

He took her around the dance floor as easily as he'd skated with her around the rink. But unlike that day, her body felt stiff and unyielding. He stared down at her, trying to find those features that had drawn him to her from day one. Her sparkling eyes, her genuine sunny smile, her light…

Now, the only bright things about her were the crown and the sparkly green dress. And they were just that. *Things.* Not his real Amber.

He began to speak, stopped, and settled for holding her in his arms. He had a feeling if he tried to talk to her, she'd cut him dead—with her ice-queen stare.

Face it. She'd accepted his invitation to dance only because she'd had to. Because she didn't want to cause a scene or to destroy the magic this night meant to her.

Becoming her King couldn't begin to excuse the way he had spoken to her this afternoon. Replacing the money Derek had stolen wouldn't get him off the hook. He'd hurt her so badly she couldn't bring herself to look at him.

He knew all that.

What he didn't know was how he could ever make up for any of it.

When the song ended, she stepped back. "Thanks for the dance," she said, her voice as brittle as her smile.

"My pleasure." But obviously not hers.

Didn't matter. His words were drowned out by the rush of congratulations from the dancers who crowded around them. By the time he'd gotten through the handshakes and hugs, Amber had disappeared.

All night, he caught only glimpses of her. He'd see her talking with her parents, helping her brothers and sisters restock the food and drinks tables, laughing with one group after another…

And never looking his way.

She didn't come near him until the grandfather clock on the stage began inching its way toward twelve. Grateful he'd at least have this last dance of the night with her, he bowed and held out his hand again. She gave him a brilliant smile, but in his arms she felt as unyielding as she had before.

When this dance ended and the crowd began to chant the countdown, he turned with her to face the stage. Wanting her with him, he kept one arm around her waist. They stood so close he could smell the light perfume she wore and see the moisture filling her eyes. Of course she'd get emotional now. This was her night and she was Queen of the Snow Ball.

What he didn't expect was his urgent need to ease her against his side. Holding her this close gave him hope the warmth of his body would somehow melt away the ice and bring his Amber back to him.

The clock struck midnight. The room filled with the sounds of applause, party horns, and cheers. Everywhere he looked, he saw handshaking and backslapping, hugs and kisses.

He turned to Amber. Her eyes were brimming, and he reached up in time to catch a stray teardrop with his fingertip, managing to stroke her soft cheek along the way. The shiver she gave left his hand shaking, too, and left him with no other choice—no other thought—but to kiss her.

As if she'd read his mind, she slipped free of his arm and fled into the crowd. In the crush of people on the dance floor, she disappeared immediately from his view.

Now he knew the worst. And it was all on him.

Not only had he hurt the woman he loved, he'd lost her forever.

• • •

The clock had struck midnight, and Cinderella had gone home with her Prince.

Well, to be precise, her King. And she hadn't actually come directly home with him. In her own car, she had gone to pick up Penny before making the drive up the mountainside. She'd arrived to find Michael had already gone upstairs. He'd called down to her, making sure she'd made the trip without any trouble. Not much comfort, but she held onto the idea that some part of him cared.

Now she stood in the middle of her housekeeper's room listening to the early-morning silence. The lodge was so quiet, so still, she and Penny might have been the only occupants. But the sound of a door closing a little while ago had told her Michael was here.

Or maybe it meant he had left.

During the night, unable to sleep, she had gone downstairs and made a batch of quick bread. She had left the cake platter, covered with a napkin, next to the coffeemaker where he would find it. It was the least she could do. But why had she felt the need to do it?

"I should have followed my instincts," she told Penny, who snuggled against her. "I never should have gone to the community center last night."

What a mess, from her awkward dance with Michael to her teary-eyed escape from the center at midnight. Just like Cinderella fleeing the ball.

Only she'd left behind more than a glass slipper.

Her attempt at a laugh sounded more like a sob. How desperate could she be, trying to find hope in a hopeless situation? How pathetic had she seemed to everyone at the ball? And how was she going to live with herself...and without Michael?

After last night's disaster, she couldn't understand why she hadn't woken up to messages on her cell phone. Not calls to congratulate her for becoming Snow Ball Queen. Or to sympathize with her for being a bad-luck Barnett sister. She didn't expect those. But Callie or Lyssa, at least, should have reached out by now to offer support…if not to point out how badly she'd messed up again.

Another check of the phone showed that, for once, it had clear reception up here.

With a sigh, she told Penny, "I probably embarrassed our entire family so much, they still haven't recovered. But I've made up my mind—I'm going to confess what happened with the electric bill. And until my next paycheck arrives, we're moving back home."

The last thing she'd ever wanted. But Michael wasn't flying home until tomorrow, and she couldn't bear to spend one more night at the lodge with him. Wherever she wound up, though, she knew where her thoughts would be.

So much for that New Year's resolution to get over him.

As she grabbed her suitcase from the bed, she glanced through the window. No sign of Michael. No rows of footprints in the snow. No tire tracks. But the blinding whiteness left her with dazzled vision.

"Oh, no," she whispered. *Not now. Please.* "We've got to get out of here."

She was halfway down the stairs when the funny but familiar buzzing began in her head. Knowing dizziness would eventually follow, she moved directly into the living room and settled Penny in her playpen. Her daughter immediately let out a cry of protest.

"Sorry, baby. Mommy needs to sit down."

"Something wrong?"

At the unexpected sound of Michael's voice, she shrieked.

"I didn't mean to startle you," he said.

"Th-that's all right. I know you didn't." She was careful not to move a muscle. But she couldn't keep from groaning. Her shriek had turned the buzzing inside her head into a steady clang.

"What's the matter?"

"Nothing. It's—I've got a migraine coming on."

A silence followed her words. Any second now, she would hear his footsteps and then the slamming of the front door.

She had been a coward for trying to leave the lodge without seeing him. So, he'd broken her heart. But what happened to her need for independence? Where was her ability to stand on her own two feet? How could slipping away prove she was a good role model for Penny?

She took a steadying breath. "I should have told you this last night, but I...didn't. Later on yesterday, Callie found a note mixed in with the checks in the cashbox." She tugged the paper from her jeans pocket and held it out to him.

He took it without a word. A second later, he muttered a curse. He didn't need to speak. She knew exactly what he was thinking. Exactly what she had thought when she'd read the note.

I HELPED MYSELF.

Michael had told Derek to start doing just that.

And indirectly or not, she had encouraged Derek to come to Snowflake Valley.

A pain shot through her temple. Groaning, she raised a shaking hand to her head.

Michael stared at her, then without a word, turned on his heel and left the room.

Her eyes misting, she swallowed hard and sank to the couch. "Baby, Mommy has to close her eyes. To take a nap, just for a few minutes." To her relief, she saw Penny was already sleeping peacefully.

She pulled the afghan from the back of the couch,

covering herself with it as she closed her eyes.

This was the worst day of her life, all over again.

This was the morning she had told her husband she was pregnant, and he had stormed out, leaving her even though he knew their argument had triggered one of her migraines. But why would he have worried about that, when he didn't even care about their baby.

This was the afternoon later that day, when she had finally felt well enough to make a trip for groceries, only to come home to find the apartment empty of everything that had belonged to him.

She took another deep breath that ended in a moan.

No, this day was so much worse. Because she loved Michael more than she had ever loved the man who had left her.

But now Michael had walked out, too. And soon she would be the one leaving and taking everything with her. Everything…including her broken heart.

Chapter Nineteen

"*Shh-h-h*, Penny," Michael said. "It's you and me right now, kid. And we've got to keep the noise level down, or we're gonna wake your mommy."

He sat in the rocking chair in the kitchen with the baby lying against his chest. Amber was still asleep in the living room. She'd slept on and off yesterday, all through last night and, so far, most of this morning. "I could have called your grandma or one of your aunts for help. You know they'd have been here in no time." Instead, he had managed on his own, dampening cloths with cool water for Amber's forehead, making tea and toast when she could finally look at food, getting bottles ready and feeding Penny.

And cancelling his flight home.

Go or stay, he had said to the baby yesterday. She'd blinked in response, but he had already made his decision.

Now, near noon, the baby was squirming against him, dealing with another bout of colic. He rocked the chair and patted her back, rocked and patted, keeping the rhythm going.

Eventually, Penny's cries eased up. When her legs rested quietly against him, he knew they'd turned a corner.

He felt glad for Amber's sake. She needed the rest, and if her baby's cries hadn't woken her by now, she would probably continue to sleep.

Truthfully, he felt glad for his and Penny's sake, too.

He set the baby on his knee, supporting her with one hand behind her head. "We're a team now, aren't we, kid. Who'd have thought it? And you know, there's strength in numbers. Between us, we've got the power to convince your mommy of a few things." He hoped.

She looked up at him, her blue eyes bright with tears—the way Amber's had been on New Year's Eve, when she'd told him about the missing money. And he had run off at the mouth and then walked out. He had let Amber believe she was responsible for what had happened, when ultimately, he was the one at fault. They had proof of that. The note she had handed him yesterday, the taunting evidence Derek had left behind, had been directed at *him*, not at Amber.

"I guess before I can convince her of anything, I'm going to have to apologize. You think?"

Penny squirmed, her face crinkling. The colic had given way to gas. He had enough experience with babies—his brothers—to know that. But he chose to take the reaction as a smile. As a good sign. "Yeah, I think so, too."

The doorbell rang.

"Da—*whoops*," he said, cutting himself off. In the future, he'd have to watch his language. For now, he could...well, he could *swear* Penny smiled again.

Laughing, he rose from the rocking chair and crossed the kitchen. "Da*whoops*, baby. That's the way it goes from now on. And we'd better go answer the door before whoever's out there wakes up your mommy."

Over on the couch, Amber looked as though she hadn't

moved a muscle.

He swung the front door open. Callie and Lyssa stood on the porch. When they saw him holding Penny, their eyes widened.

He clutched the baby to him. *Dawhoops, all right.*

"Is Amber—" Lyssa began.

"*Shh-h-h*," he hissed. "Asleep on the couch."

"Migraine?" Callie asked in a low voice.

He nodded and led the way to the kitchen.

While they stood taking off their gloves and jackets, he settled Penny in her carrier on the kitchen table. "Coffee? Cake?" he asked.

"You're quite the host," Lyssa said. "Nick should take notes."

"Amber made the cake," he admitted. "But I'm handy with the coffeepot."

"And with babies." Callie smiled.

"We'll pass on the refreshments," Lyssa said. "We're not staying long," she added as the three of them took seats. "Unless you need some help."

He shook his head.

Callie turned to him. "Sorry for barging in on you, but Nick said you were leaving today. We tried Amber's cell and the lodge phone this morning, but didn't get an answer. Nick didn't know when your flight was, so we tried you, too, but no luck."

"I disconnected the lodge phone," he explained, "and turned off both the cells so the ring wouldn't wake Amber."

The two women exchanged a glance. He tensed, but before he could continue, Lyssa said, "Has she been sleeping since yesterday?"

"Most of the time, yeah. I think it's half from the migraine and half just from being the mom of a baby with colic. I've been keeping Penny occupied."

Lyssa and Callie exchanged another glance.

"You're one heck of a nice guy," Lyssa said, "and much better than the one Amber married."

"Why?" he blurted. Out of politeness, he probably should have protested some of that statement. Oh, well.

"The day her ex walked out on her," Callie said quietly, "Amber started with a migraine. He knew how they affected her. He left, anyway."

He swore, but under his breath. "What a louse."

"We thought that, too."

"Yeah." He paused, then went for it. "As for being 'better than the one Amber married,' I have to tell you, I'm not—"

"Michael." Lyssa rested her hand on his arm. "You don't have to tell us anything. Neither does Amber." She grinned. "But I need to inform *you*, if you two don't settle things between you soon, the Barnett family is going to have another conference."

"Or an intervention," Callie said.

"We'll be talking," he promised.

"Good. Anyhow, we drove up, first of all, to find out if everything was okay."

"It is," he said firmly. "And I want to know how things worked out about the auction."

To their credit, neither woman tried to evade him.

Lyssa said, "That's the other reason we're here."

"Since my parents are co-chairs of the festival," Callie said, "and the auction was an offshoot of it, we decided to keep what happened all in the family. We held a conference this afternoon."

"Why am I not surprised?" he asked.

The women laughed.

"A conference minus Amber, of course," Lyssa said. "But we're sure we know her vote. And not one of us thinks you should be penalized for something Derek did."

"I can afford to make the donation. Besides," he muttered, "he's my brother." *And I drove him to it.*

Callie shook her head. "You're not responsible for anyone else's action, even a member of your family. As for being able to afford the donation..." She smiled. "We all agree that's true, and we thank you for the offer. Which we're happy to accept. The auction money will stay intact, the school will get exactly what we earned, and all will be well in Snowflake Valley."

No. All wouldn't be well in this town until he talked with Amber.

• • •

Amber woke to the sound of voices. Startled, she sat up.

No buzzing, no banging, no dizziness. Her migraine had subsided. She looked quickly at the playpen. It was empty. As she rose from the couch, she heard another voice. What was Callie doing here?

As she neared the kitchen, she heard Callie again.

"I think we all agree we're done here. So if you're still sure you don't need our help, we'll be on our way."

"Thanks, but no, thanks," Michael said. "We're all doing fine. Penny and I have come to an agreement of our own. And Amber's still sleeping. We'll let her rest until she's good and ready to wake up again."

Amber cleared her throat.

Everyone in the kitchen, including Penny, looked toward the doorway.

"I'm awake," she said.

"So we see," Callie returned.

She and Lyssa looked at one another. Amber knew those expressions well. Her two oldest sisters were up to something. But to her surprise, they both simply put on their jackets and gloves and took turns leaning over the baby seat to kiss Penny.

Then they were gone in a flurry of words—*good-bye* and *call you tomorrow* and *make sure you eat and get more rest*—and Amber was left alone with Penny and Michael.

She wanted to sit near them but didn't dare. Getting so close to Michael would make her lose her nerve. Instead, she took a seat opposite them.

"How about some soup?" he asked. "That's about all I have here, besides your cake."

"I'd love some soup. Even canned soup. Isn't this where you came in last week?" she asked, hoping he would smile. He didn't.

"Sounds like it. And judging by your packed suitcase in the living room, you intended to leave yesterday."

She watched him move comfortably from cabinet to cabinet, knowing where to find the soup and the saucepan, the bowl and the ladle. And just think, until a few days ago he'd never cooked in this kitchen.

Until a few days ago, he'd never touched her or kissed her. And yet she'd loved him long before then.

He turned from the stove. "Is your electricity on again?"

"No."

"So you can't have been headed to your apartment. Not without heat. Where were you going to stay?"

"At home. With my family."

"You didn't want them to know about your financial situation."

"No, I didn't."

"Then why were you leaving?"

"Because..." She'd planned to tell him calmly and quietly how she felt, but other, uncontrollable emotions took over and the words tumbled out. "Because I don't want to stay here. I can't. I can't be with you, knowing I'm just your housekeeper and cook. Or just your fake date. I don't want to be your fake anything, Michael. Because I love you."

He took a deep breath. "Amber, I can't—"

"I know. Don't say it," she whispered. She *did* know—all the reasons they couldn't be "together." Why he couldn't love her. Why she had to get over loving him. "I can't expect you to feel the way I do. But I hope you can at least forgive me about what happened. With Derek, I mean."

"There's nothing to forgive."

"But if I hadn't talked to him about the festival, he'd never have come here."

"Yes, he would have. He wasn't out for fun and games. He wanted money and then to get back at me. Just his good luck, he managed both at once. Considering the note he wrote throwing my words at me, I blamed myself, too. But when your sisters showed up this morning, Callie said something that made the truth kick in. She said we're not responsible for someone else's actions, even when it's someone in our own family."

"Callie's very intelligent."

"You are, too. You'd already told me the same thing she had, but in different words."

"I thought the idea sounded familiar."

"And somehow, I know you're not going to take the credit for it." He smiled.

He smiled.

Call her a fool, but a tiny shiver of hope ran through her. When he turned to stir the soup, she reached over to adjust Penny's pajama cuff.

"Hey, baby," she whispered. "Mommy loves you."

And Mommy loves Michael.

In the past twenty-four-plus-hours, she had done more than sleep. She'd seen what Michael had been up to. Taking care of her. Looking after Penny. Staying in Snowflake Valley, when by now he should have been in San Diego. All that had to mean something. And it told her she couldn't walk away without giving her hopes and dreams one more shot at success.

Michael set the bowl of soup in front of her. "I have to tell you, intelligence must run in your family. Lyssa's pretty darned smart, too. And so is Penny."

"Does that have something to do with the agreement you and she made?"

For a moment, his brows crinkled in a frown. Then he laughed. "You heard that?"

"Yes. Well...overheard it."

"We did come to an agreement," he said. "A few, in fact. We did a lot of talking while you were sleeping."

She moved the soup bowl aside. How could she eat when her hopes and dreams hung in the balance?

Michael eyed the bowl but said nothing about it. "First, Penny and I decided I owed you an apology. I admit, I let the situation about Derek get away from me. Partly because he'd stolen the money, but mostly because I thought you'd arranged a reunion, even after everything I'd said about my family. I'm sorry."

She nodded. "Apology accepted."

"Good. Second, we concluded you nailed it with everything on my brothers. Not everyone is like Derek. Raymond and Lee are...good kids. They're my only half-brothers, and just as you said, I *was* closer to them growing up. And they're all different people."

"You and Penny figured all this out together, huh?"

"We did. And the list goes on." Shrugging, he stared down at the table. "I guess me going off to college was like you getting your apartment—a way to prove my independence. Being away from home made it easier to deny I had ties to any of my family."

"That's not my reason for wanting to live on my own."

"Agreed. That's not you. It would never be you." He smiled briefly. "But for me, not admitting a connection meant that whenever Carmen's kids got out of hand, it was okay to walk away. I'm sorry about that now, too. Especially because of Raymond and Lee."

"It's not too late. You've made a good start in building some bridges to them."

"Again, thanks to you. I'm happy for that and plan to continue. But right now, I'm focused on building something with you and Penny." With every word he spoke, more pieces of her broken heart mended. When he took her hand, she squeezed his fingers in silent encouragement. "Being around the baby, taking care of her, brought back a lot of memories of babysitting for the boys. But not just that. Remember I told you that when I was growing up, my dad worked almost all the time?"

She nodded.

"He needed the overtime to support us. I realize that now. Back then, I thought he just didn't want to be a father. That, like me in college, he walked away by staying at work. I blamed him and I blamed my stepmother and her messed-up kids for a whole list of things. But now I—Penny and I—figured out the truth."

"Which is…?"

"Some of my own thinking was messed up, too. Because I never had my dad around to show me the ropes, I thought I couldn't be a good dad or raise a family. And because I never knew what a real family was like, I convinced myself I never wanted one of my own."

Her rapidly healing heart raced. "And now?"

"Now, I've met your family and have seen some truths about mine. And just as you said about people, not every family is alike."

Michael's happiness was her happiness. Were his hopes

the same as hers? "Are you planning to act on any of these insights?"

"Are you asking if I want a family of my own?"

"I'm asking if you want *my* family."

He tilted his head, as if he needed to think about his answer.

"No teasing now," she warned. "No pretending."

"Does calling you my Queen count?"

"*Michael.*" She clasped her hands together. "Oh, pretty please…"

He laughed. "Fight dirty all you want, Amber. Nothing could distract me now."

"Or me. Not when I'm fighting to win something I've wanted all my life."

"Then, game over, sweetheart." He came around the table and tugged her to her feet. "I love you, Amber. I love you and Penny. And I feel pretty good about the rest of the Barnetts."

She laughed.

He slid his arms around her waist and held her close. "Thanks to you—and your brilliant daughter—I've realized the truth. I do want a family. A big, loving, supportive family. And what could be better than one that's ready-made for me? So, the short answer to this long speech… Yes, I want *your* family."

Suddenly, his expression grew so solemn, her heart skipped a beat.

"I want a family of our own, too," he said quietly. "And I promise you, Amber, I'll be the best dad I can be to Penny and the rest of our kids."

Her eyes blurred and her throat tightened and she couldn't manage a word. She couldn't believe her luck. Her *good* luck.

As if Michael had heard the response she couldn't make,

he leaned down to kiss her—a long, sweet, satisfying kiss that sealed his promise.

When he finally raised his head and looked at her again, it took a while to find her breath, to realize she had just been handed her hopes and dreams, all wrapped up with a big red bow. "I want that big family, too. But…"

He stilled. "But what? If you're not ready to get married yet, I'll wait. I'll wait forever if I have to."

"Oh, it won't take that long. I'd marry you today." She smiled through her tears. "I'm just wondering how many kids you'd like to have."

Epilogue

Four days later…

"Are you ready for this, Penny?" For the ninety-ninth time this morning, Amber glanced at the bedside clock in the housekeeper's room. Michael had made her promise she would stay upstairs until the stroke of eight. "Time for us to find out what's been going on."

He had extended his Snowflake Valley vacation indefinitely. For the first couple of days, they had almost barricaded themselves inside the lodge, just the three of them. Part of that time, he had concentrated on his project for the town council. The bids wouldn't be due for a while, but he'd wanted to get started on the job. She'd been thrilled to see him so eager about doing the work he loved.

Yesterday, he had become very secretive. Taking private phone calls. Closing his office door. Making solo trips down to the valley.

She was only human. She couldn't help but wonder what he was up to. Wonder, but not worry. Michael was a man she could count on.

Smiling, she went downstairs with Penny. At the bottom of the staircase, she stared in amazement. *She* was the one famous in Snowflake Valley for her parties and her decorating skills. But it seemed Michael had been getting in a little practice.

Everywhere she looked, she saw lights and tinsel and bright, shiny decorations.

Michael had insisted he didn't mind her leaving the Christmas tree in the corner through Little Christmas. Today. As she looked at the tree, her eyes blurred. He had replaced all the ornaments she had hung with handmade snowflakes covered in glitter.

"Made especially for you," he said, "with an extra helping of elf magic dust." His voice came from behind her, but she couldn't tear her gaze from the tree. "Do you like it?" he asked.

"I love it," she said, fighting and failing to blink away her tears. She turned and found him standing in the doorway near the dining area. With that once glance, her tears overflowed.

He was dressed head-to-toe as Santa.

As she wiped at her cheeks with the back of her hand, he crossed the room. He reached for Penny, who went to him with outstretched arms and patted his white beard. "I've banished Scrooge. And luckily, Callie and Lyssa knew where I could get this outfit. What do you think? Do I make a good Santa?"

"The best," she whispered, her voice breaking.

He thumbed a tear from her cheek. "It's a few days late, I know. But I wanted Penny's first Christmas to be our first real Christmas together. And I wanted it to be magical. For you."

"Oh, *Michael*." She looked at him through another sudden haze.

From outside, she heard the sound of car doors slamming,

followed by the murmur of voices and a laugh.

"I invited your whole gang to spend the day with us," he said. "Hope that's all right."

"It's perfect." She smiled. "After all, Christmas wouldn't be Christmas without family."

About the Author

Barbara White Daille is an award-winning author whose short contemporary romances have received Top Picks and glowing reviews. Her books focus on small-town settings, where the heroes and heroines' lives are filled with family and friends, lots of nosy neighbors, and often a matchmaker—or three.

Barbara has been a writer since before she could spell all the words in her stories. She and her husband live in the hot and sunny Southwest, where they love the lizards in the front yard but could do without the scorpions in the bathroom.

Discover the* Snowflake Valley *series…

SNOWBOUND WITH MR. WRONG

Find your Bliss with these great releases...

FOUR WEDDINGS AND A FLING

a *Weddings in Westchester* novel by Barbara DeLeo

Grace Bennett is determined to set a perfect example for her new wedding planning business. From now on it will take more than good looks and a charming smile to win her over. The next guy to get her attention will be sweet, dependable, and looking for something serious. But first she'll have to survive the next couple of weeks at The Aegean Palace with swoon-worthy Ari Katsalos. Ari and Grace want very different things, but it's getting tough to resist the powerful chemistry burning between them.

A HUSBAND BY NEW YEAR'S

a *McClendon Holiday* novel by Sean D. Young

Renee wants a regular guy who's not afraid to get his hands dirty, and she's given herself a deadline. If she doesn't find Mr. Right by New Year's, she's done searching. Patrick wants is a woman who'll want him for who is, and not only see dollar signs, so when he hits it off with Renee, he doesn't tell her everything. But when the truth comes out, how forgiving will Renee be?

HER SURPRISE ENGAGEMENT

a *Sorensen* novel by Ashlee Mallory

All single mom Daisy Sorensen wants is to enjoy a much-needed, stress-free family vacation at a friend's Lake Tahoe home. So of course a gorgeous man and his daughter show up in the middle of the night. When things spiral out of control the next morning, Jack makes Daisy an offer she can't refuse. But in between late-night campfires and days on the lake, Jake finds himself falling for the strong, stubborn woman for real.

Made in the USA
Middletown, DE
03 April 2025

73727126R00122